FIRST PROOF

FIRST PROOF

THE PENGUIN BOOK OF NEW WRITING FROM INDIA 3

PENGUIN BOOKS

PENGUIN BOOKS
Penguin Books India Pvt. Ltd, 11 Community Centre, Panchsheel Park,
New Delhi 110 017, India
Penguin Group (USA) Inc., 375 Hudson Street, New York, New York 10014, USA
Penguin Group (Canada), 90 Eglinton Avenue East, Suite 700, Toronto, Ontario,
M4P 2Y3, Canada (a division of Pearson Penguin Canada Inc.)
Penguin Books Ltd, 80 Strand, London WC2R 0RL, England
Penguin Ireland, 25 St Stephen's Green, Dublin 2, Ireland
(a division of Penguin Books Ltd)
Penguin Group (Australia), 250 Camberwell Road, Camberwell,
Victoria 3124, Australia (a division of Pearson Australia Group Pty Ltd)
Penguin Group (NZ), 67 Apollo Drive, Rosedale, North Shore 0632, New Zealand
(a division of Pearson New Zealand Ltd)
Penguin Group (South Africa) (Pty) Ltd, 24 Sturdee Avenue, Rosebank,
Johannesburg 2196, South Africa

Penguin Books Ltd, Registered Offices: 80 Strand, London WC2R 0RL, England

First published by Penguin Books India 2007

Anthology copyright © Penguin Books India 2007
Copyright for individual pieces vests with the individual authors.

All rights reserved

10 9 8 7 6 5 4 3 2 1

ISBN-13: 978-0-14310-244-1   ISBN-10: 0-14310-244-3

Cover photograph and design by Pinaki De

Typeset in *Adobe Garamond* by SÜRYA, New Delhi
Printed at Pauls Press, New Delhi

Dedicated to the memory of Shakti Bhatt
who, sadly, didn't live to see her story published.

NON-FICTION

Contents

1   **Chasing Nyima**
SANKAR SRIDHAR

13   **My Lovely Restaurant**
SHANKAR SHARMA

23   **The Sufi Way in Malerkotla**
NIRUPAMA DUTT

45   **One Day in DC**
ASHOK MALIK

51   **Musings on a Mobike**
PALDEN GYALSTEN

58   **Fouta Unbound**
KRITI SHARMA

68   **Can't Please Anyone**
SHUBHRA GUPTA

81   **Khullam Khulla**
AMAN SETHI

93   **Father-in-law Has Pots of Money**
AVIJIT GHOSH

106   **Notes on Contributors**

CONTRIBUTORS TO *FIRST PROOF*

VOLUME 1

Sarnath Banerjee * Ritu Bhatia * Alban Couto * Mamang Dai *
Rana Dasgupta * Mita Ghose * Indrajit Hazra * Ranjit Hoskote *
Arun John * Uma Mahadevan-Dasgupta * Palash Krishna Mehrotra *
Renuka Narayanan * Anuradha Roy * Mitali Saran * Navtej Sarna *
Ambarish Satwik * Paromita Vohra * André Béteille * Saba
Naqvi Bhaumik * Arpita Das * Sunanda K. Datta-Ray * Edna
Fernandes * Naresh Fernandes * Smita Gupta * Manmohan
Malhoutra * Jerry Pinto * Mishi Saran * Ajai Shukla * Nirupama
Subramanian * Sankarshan Thakur

VOLUME 2

C. Sriram * Sampurna Chattarji * Chandrahas Choudhury * Soumitro
Das * Sonia Faleiro * Dhruba Hazarika * K. Srilata * Rahul
Karmakar * Vivek Narayanan * E.V. Ramakrishnan * Anushka
Ravishankar * Satyajit Sarna * Manreet Sodhi Someshwar * Kanishk
Tharoor * Altaf Tyrewala * Annie Zaidi * Samrat Choudhury *
Dilip D'Souza * Salman Haidar * Manju Kak * Smriti Nevatia *
Sheela Reddy * Ranjana Sengupta * Pepita Seth * Arunava Sinha *
Sanjay Suri * Jeet Thayil

Chasing Nyima

SANKAR SRIDHAR

Chasing after girls is not my strong suit, especially not at 5 a.m. when the temperature by my trusty watch is a teeth-chattering eight below freezing. The lack of oxygen at 14,000 feet and that Nyima is indulging in some laughter therapy at my expense isn't helping either.

Had it not been for the stubborn incline between her and me, I would have wrung her neck. Had it not been for the million miles separating us, I would have shaken the sun out of its slumber and ordered it to shine, had I not seen the moisture from my breath frost over and settle on my whiskers, I would have wept like a baby. I would have, but did not. Instead, I continue walking in excruciating slow motion, eyes glued to Nyima. The last thing I want is to get lost. This land is so bare it makes the sky, scattered with cauliflower clouds, look crowded. And I am not the first one feeling this in the Changtang, the sandy plains of Ladakh that melt into the western edge of the Tibetan plateau. When translated, the name means 'the vast nothingness'.

It's a name that was, perhaps, coined by the Changpa, nomadic herdsmen of Tibetan stock who, by some records, are considered the first people to have arrived here some centuries ago and with whom I intend to spend a week, once I find them.

Nyima says we will reach her father's *rebo* (a Changpa's tent) today. She had said that yesterday as well, minutes before I traded the comfort of a car, the camaraderie of my friend Rashid and even the safety of a tent, for the fifteen-year-old's company at Hanle (pronounced A-ng-le), where I chanced to meet her at the monastery.

For the uninitiated, the valley of Hanle is around 240 km from Leh, the capital of Ladakh—and 19 km from India's disputed border with China. A road leads up to an army checkpost at Mahe, but beyond that you need to trust the tyre marks left on the sand by army vehicles or your instincts if you are unlucky enough to have a storm wipe away the trail. In the rolling plains beyond, life has changed little.

Even today, the 3,000-odd families that scour the valleys for pasture remain the only permanent inhabitants—that's if you leave out the army personnel posted there. And now, after walking for almost twenty hours in two days and spending the night in between shivering in a sleeping bag under an open sky, I know why.

It's tough being a nomad, tougher still if you come from the plains, with plain lungs, and plain legs whose idea of exercise is to stretch after the rest of the body wakes up each morning.

For her thin-as-a barley-stalk frame, Nyima packs quite a punch. But that's because she was born, like all other Changpas, with lungs that are double the size of mine. A lifetime of walking this sea of sand helped her perfect a difficult-to-duplicate demeanour of walking. She's swift and light-footed and her gait exudes an energy-saving economy of movement. I can make out that she can continue walking for miles on end and still have energy to spare to laugh at my misery. The thought does little to boost my spirits.

I try reminding myself that meeting Changpas was not part

2

of my original plan, console myself by picturing a shocked Nyima standing at a city thoroughfare not knowing when to cross, while I do so effortlessly and laugh hysterically at her suffering. I hope such thoughts will fill me with the sadistic pleasure that will take away some of my pain. It does not.

Without options, I wash down my pride with a mouthful of water, clear my throat and croak—'*Ruko*' just as the sun clears the rim of a mountain and drenches the valley in a splash of light. Where there was soggy darkness a second ago, now there is colour. I drag myself to where Nyima has stopped and sprawl out. As the sun warms my blood and my breath begins to even out, I take in my surroundings. Avalanching slopes rush down to meet a lake so blue it seems a swathe of sky has come crashing down. Tufts of grass burnt yellow and brown by the sun pepper the land all the way to the horizon, where the skyline is creased by corrugated cliffs that remind me of what the readings of an ECG machine would have looked like had its wires been clipped to my chest moments ago. And for the first time my eyes rest on that blotch of black.

Over the next three hours, the blotch grows and new shapes begin to emerge— cloud-like tufts floating around and a strange streak of buff that zips among them once in a while—until I am close enough to identify them all. The black rebo, the grazing sheep and that streak of buff, now flying straight at me: a rabid dog.

It is in this moment of pure blood-freezing terror that another shape emerges from the tent and from its pursed lips emerges a shrill whistle. It's the dog's turn to freeze, a metre from my calves.

'*Julley! Namastey!*' I hear the man say as he hobbles up to the

3

dog and, lifting its forepaws, loops them into its collar to immobilize it. He then introduces himself as Urghyen, Nyima's father, and invites me to stay even before I can make my request.

Urghyen is a raw-boned man of around fifty who uses a rusted blade and nothing else to shave his stubble every other day. He spends most of his waking hours telling a rosary. He says his daughter means the world to him, especially since the cold claimed his wife two years ago and the scorching sun robbed him of most of his eyesight some years before that.

Like the topography that has cradled an ancient way of life and has at once relegated the tribe to an existence without even the rudimentary elements of comforts and cures, the sun is a blessing and a curse in the high trans-Himalaya. It melts the ice, makes rivers flow, helps the grass grow and all life flourish, but its ultra-violet rays also singes the skin and ruins the retina.

But Urghyen, like the other Changpas, doesn't spare such trivialities much thought. It's a moksha-esque acceptance of whatever comes their way—life, death, misery or misfortune. For them everything is about Karma, and for the better. The only time they do complain is when the days are exceptionally sunny and the temperatures soar to above 30 degrees Celsius. On a day like today.

We retreat into the rebo to discuss my role in the adopted family. But first we have tea, served in porcelain cups, one of the few things modern that the Changpas have embraced. Others include Chinese blankets, jackets, shoes and, in one wealthy Changpa family I met at Hanle, a scooter with licence plates of Chandigarh. Hindi, too, is a language they have recently learnt, thanks to their interaction with the army. But such possessions do little to reduce hardship. So after learning that my job will

4

include walking up to sixteen hours each day with the sheep, and collecting their scat on the way, I tuck myself into the sleeping bag for the hardship that lies ahead.

It is late evening when I wake up. The wind has picked up, the temperature has dipped, the goats have been corralled, milked and a not-so-lucky-one slaughtered by a butcher who had come to buy a few of them. The killing, I learn, was in my honour.

The Changpas' staple is meat, but being Buddhists they don't shed blood. In the past, Urghyen told me, they would plug a goat's nose and wait. 'Yaks, we would strap their mouth with rope and wait till they starved.'

That takes around twenty days. Nowadays visiting butchers do them, and the animals, a favour. Dinner was boiled goat intestine filled with goat blood. The Changpas also eat roast meat, boiled meat, raw meat, meat dried and coated with salt, dried meat ground into flour and carried in leather pouches and eaten all day. Yes, I have tried them all, but that's another story.

I wake up to screaming winds, chaotic snowflakes and an icy hand on my shoulder the next morning. It's time to wake up, Urghyen says, handing me a cup of butter tea.

A needling cold that drills itself through wool and skin and into the bone greets me outside of the tent. It's snowing so heavily, I can't even see my outstretched hand, but Nyima tells me it's time to go. I'm horrified, but for Urghyen, Nyima and the Changpas like them, this is no hardship. It's part of the natural cycle.

By the time I wrap myself with wool, feathers and an assortment of clothes to keep the cold at bay, Nyima removes the wooden frame that blocks the corral's exit. After milking the goats, Urghyen busies himself collecting their droppings. It's precious fuel that will help them survive another winter.

It's so cold outside, even the shaggy dog shows no aggression. It yawns, I follow suit. It breaks into a trot after the goats and the girl. I wish I could.

But for the storm, which exhausted itself in three hours, it is an easy day, for the girl can't hurry the goats as they nibble on the meagre resources. Winter is setting in and any goat not fit or fat enough won't survive. To make matters worse, a plague of locusts had descended on vast swathes of the valleys this year, and by the time the cold killed them off, there was not much left for the goats. 'That's why I had gone to Hanle *gonpa* (monastery),' Nyima tells me. 'To pray for the goats and yak.'

For this tribe, which lives at the mercy of the vagaries of weather, prayers are a way of life. And what we might classify as a miracle—such as the freak snowstorm that killed the locusts—is just a reaffirmation of faith to them.

It took us three days, in which time we crossed a nameless pass and skirted a nameless lake and passed through nameless, featureless lands—to finally come to a place that had a name. Chumur. The days in between had been idle. Nyima occasionally dipped into her bag, took out a fistful of *tsampa* (barley flour), mixed it with a bowl of water and drank it up, or wolfed down several forms of meat. I nibbled at biscuits or chocolates. She refused them, just as she refused to be photographed. The rest of the time she was either whistling to her dog, swirling her sling, made from the hairs of a horse's tail, and throwing stones at straggling sheep or running to some secret spring to fill her bottle. Just as the sun set, she would tie up the goats' feet to keep them from wandering and slink into the yak-hair blanket she carried on her back all day. The dog did the guarding and he was good at it.

On the fourth day, as the sun melted the icicles formed along a stream, I finally decide to break the ice. I click her picture, and even before she can complain, show it to her. She's thrilled. '*Aur hain* (do you have any more)?' she asks. I show her. By the end of the hour, she has asked me for biscuits, has made me a bowl of the paste to taste and has offered to share all she has in her bag. With his master my friend now, the dog, too, sniffs me out and gives me a reluctant wag of his tail. He gets a biscuit for the effort.

I, too, don't feel tired any more. Perhaps it has to do with acclimatization, or perhaps my city carapace is peeling off with the rest of my singed skin. I feel so fit I could trek all the way to some brackish-water lake, collect salt, load them on to horses and head off to Kashgar in China, just like the Changpas did in the days of the Silk Route trade.

For now, however, we are just heading back. I was still a lot slower than Nyima was and still had trouble getting the whistle shrill enough to attract the dog's attention, but Nyima's smile suggested I was well and truly on my way to turning Changpa.

It's time for celebration when we get back to the rebo, my home, on Day Six.

Urghyen knew I would weather the journey well and had already prepared *Chhang* (a heady brew made by fermenting barley, which the Changpa barter for wool and meat in villages) to mark the baptism. He would call me *Thamo* (the thin one) from this day on. I am truly family now.

As we drink bowl after bowl of chaang, to mark my transformation from city-slicker to Changpa, I can't help but ask if Urghyen ever tired of this life.

7

'Why?'

'It's so much hard work. The weather is so unpredictable, doesn't it get lonely?'

Urghyen laughs, his face breaking into a thousand wrinkles.

'The grass grows by itself, the goats and yak eat them, reproduce and stay healthy all by themselves. We get whatever we want—milk, meat, clothes—from them. We do nothing, and you call this a hard life!'

I'm stunned by the simplicity of this truth.

'As for the unpredictability of Chantang's weather, we are very afraid,' Urghyen says. 'My wife lived forty-five winters before making a mistake. She was not forgiven.'

But the nomads have honed skills of surviving the winters well. The yak-hair tents they weave provide great insulation and also provide enough ventilation to keep it cool on the hottest of days. The yak-hair quilts can keep them warm even in a snowstorm. They follow traditional routes to hidden pastures to keep their herds healthy.

'We don't try to control the Changtang, but try to understand it so we can keep ourselves and our home healthy.'

It's a strategy tested by time itself. By rotating the pastures, the nomads ensure they never overgraze a patch. The milk, made into cheese and butter forms their staple, along with meat, and helps them during the long seven months when the Changtang is sealed by snow. And a stash of fodder, cut, bundled and stocked just before winter sets in, helps keep the herds alive.

The Changpa are also choosy about the sheep they choose for the slaughter. The old and the weak are the first to go; it's a culling that not only ensures a steady supply of food, but also healthy offspring. The knowledge has been passed down from generation to generation. Urghyen learnt everything that he does from his father and will in turn, pass on his skills to his son, though he's unsure whether he will ever put them to good use.

'He wants to go the city, away from our home. He hears stories from some of the others who have done so. They come wearing different clothes and he wants them. He asks his friends to ask their friends to get him clothes like the ones you wear.'

I come to know that Urghyen has already lost a son to the glitz of the town that is Leh and the lure of lucre and an 'easy life'.

Karma, Urghyen says, worked as a porter, unloading sacks of rice and wheat from trucks and depositing them in the godown adjoining a ration shop. His only concern is that his younger son, too, will follow, leading a life of bondage.

'We are nomads and should be proud of it,' Urghyen tells me. 'As long as we have sheep and the Changtang has grass, we will stay here and we will be free.'

Nyima's brother, as Urghyen refers to his prodigal younger son Temba, is only seven years old and was visiting a friend's rebo two days in a different direction when I had arrived. I meet him the next day. Temba studies in the primary school at Hanle.

The government, Indian and Chinese, have been unsuccessful in trying to make the Changpas give up their nomadic lifestyle. Houses built for them are shunned by most. But increasingly, they have begun to realize the value of education, the reason why most Changpa children go to school and learn their ancient ways during vacations.

Temba's school will reopen in three days, I am told. He will leave with his uncle, Lobsang, the day after tomorrow. On horseback.

'Do you have an extra horse which I could ride to Mahe?' I ask. I am due to meet Rashid (my Ladakhi friend whose vehicle I was travelling in before meeting Nyima) there in four days.

Urghyen's reply would roughly translate to: 'A Changpa without a horse is like a man without manhood.'

I took it to be a 'Yes.'

After spending most of the next day listening to Urghyen's exploits—from wrangling with snow leopards to crossing over into China—and explaining how a person who did not raise sheep could earn a living and how the sun does not actually touch the ground in the plains, where there are no mountains for it to hide behind, I have dinner and wish everyone good night.

Lobsang arrives around 8 am the next day. Urghyen has, by this time, brought a shiny white steed and shown me how to handle the skittish creature. After a hushed discussion between the two, I am told Lobsang will escort me to Mahe and return with the horse.

I accept an assortment of meats as a parting present and give Urghyen my stock of chocolate and biscuits and my sunglasses to keep. As we ready to head for Hanle, Urghyen and Nyima busy themselves packing their tent. With winter just a few squalls away, they will be heading to lower reaches of the Changtang— tent, herds, utensils and all—to where the weather is less harsh and grass buried under the snow is within muzzle-shuffling reach of the sheep. Urghyen and Nyima, too, will be tested. In the bleak months of winter, very little separates life from death. These people, like their livestock, will have to ration their stores well. A shortage of fuel, food or warm layers of sheep and yak wool could be disastrous. I had seen Urghyen taking stock— counting the sacks of dung and droppings, carefully packing the meat and barley flour—and was relieved by the look of satisfaction on his face.

It would take them an hour or so to pack up and leave. Once they set off, the only signs of their seasonal sojourn would be the darkened patch where the hearth burned. Then the land would heal, cocooned under the icy grip of winter, just like it had for millennia and come alive once again in the short spring, ready to welcome Urghyen, his daughter and their sheep.

In an hour, we were on top of the hill from which I had first seen the rebo. Looking back one last time, I spotted the line cloud-like tufts, that speck of brown and two upright dots following the train.

Dismounting from the horse, we led them downhill. 'Will Urghyen return to this place next year?' I asked Lobsang.

'If the winter spares him.'

No one spoke after that in the eight hours that it took us to reach Hanle.

We rested in the shelter of a smaller, but equally warm tent that night, Temba fast asleep, Lobsang heady on chhang and I tripping on the week I spent with Urghyen and Nyima.

After dropping Temba off at school the next day, we made for Mahe, lunching on the bank of a lake where a pair of black-necked cranes were courting, and having dinner in the light of a candle, the full moon and a million twinkles. It was a setting that lent itself to the grief of parting.

A wayward cloud shed some snow, reminding us that we needed to hurry to Mahe.

'You will return to your world tomorrow,' Lobsang told me, 'and we to ours. Don't forget us, Thamo. Wherever we are, we won't forget you.'

It is around 2 pm the next day when we finally reach Mahe. Once I am done showing the army personnel my passport and permit, Lobsang excuses himself for a moment and dives behind a cluster of rocks and shrubs after handing me the reins of the horses. As I stand there waiting for Rashid, a vehicle stuffed with four foreign tourists approaches. They leap out and head straight for me. 'Julley photo!?' one of them shouts. I smile and nod my head. He points to the horses and, miming the way of mounting them, smiles at me. I decide to give him a photograph worth framing, or, perhaps, even worth the cover of a magazine. I stand on the horse, just like Lobsang had shown me the day before.

Cameras click wildly, there are smiles all around. One of the tourists calls me and shows me my photo on the LCD screen of his camera.

I almost can't recognize myself. I do look like a Changpa. My skin is burned, my hair is raging like a blizzard on my head, my clothes are creased with sweat and dirt and my outspread hands are calloused.

The tourist fishes out a candy bar and hands it to me. It's the essential reward for local people who behave well and pose better.

I want to say 'thank you', but stop myself before the words escape my mouth.

I am Thamo, the Changpa.

I say '*Tashi Delek*' instead.

My Lovely Restaurant

SHANKAR SHARMA

For an undesirably lengthy though not unbearably long period
(i.e. for more than a week but for less than a decade) I served as
a part-time waiter in a rather dodgy Indian restaurant in Scotland.

Granted, there are less palatable occupations: abattoir
attendant; dog food-taster; proctologist; bikini-waxer (for elderly
ladies) etc. And being a waiter does at least allow one to utilize
labour in some minor way for society's benefit rather than being
a lecherous source of income: management consultancy; public
relations; human resources etc. Yet, nobody's going to laud you
for your Joycean narrative, Tolstoyan plot, Dickensian
characterization or Proustian prose when there's a fly in their
soup. Or worse still, when their soup's on your flies.

This rather dodgy Indian restaurant rests not so peacefully
in front of a graveyard in my hometown. My hometown bears
the same dreary appearance and humdrum soporific atmosphere
of many dull inconsequential little Scottish towns. Don't be
fooled! It really is a dull inconsequential little town.

As for the restaurant, it greets you on the outside with the
sight of a dilapidated refrigerator, smashed windowpanes, rusting
empty drums and overturned cardboard boxes. Upon first entry,
the sticky carpet, fused light bulbs and tacky posters make you
feel as though you have entered a cheap and nasty establishment.
Don't be fooled! It really is a cheap and nasty establishment.

Like perhaps the majority of Indian restaurants in the UK,

it is owned, run and managed by cowboys rather than Indians. In this case the ladle and spatula-slingers hailed from the wild west of the Pakistan Punjab. Urdu and Punjabi were therefore the lingua francas. For staff members unable to converse in either tongue (such as yours truly) communication was rendered possible via a smattering of English, wild gesturing and a relentless stream of expletives. It never ceased to boggle my Pakistani overlords, however, that an individual could look subcontinental, bear a subcontinental name, yet be unable to speak Urdu or Punjabi. Needless to say that none of them knew anything about Assam or the North-East of India. Or even India for that matter. That was just some place east of Punjab.

'Shankar! Why you no speak Punjabi?'

''Cos I'm not Punjabi.'

'No Punjabi?! Why you no speak Urdu then?'

'Why you no speak English?'

'I speak English very nice. Now @*#% off outside and speak nice to customer.'

Such effervescent dialogue was part and parcel. Still, if one can't stand the heat then...

'Get out @*#%-ing kitchen!'

... which is exactly what I strived for as much as possible during the course of a night's work. It can after all be quite arduous to placate someone through clear logical reasoning when they're wielding a meat cleaver in one hand, and a white-hot skewer plucked in the other.

Having said that, the kitchen was a fascinating place. Especially for criminologists. Just how many examples of illegal practice could one find within such narrow confines? Perhaps that question should be rephrased. Just how many examples of legal practice could one find within such narrow confines? Not many.

The cooks who were spoiling the broth had all been smuggled in through the back of frozen food vans. One wanders what enticements would have been sold to them and their families back home. *Come to Britain! We can huddle several of you in the same squalid flat! We can offer plenty of jobs in grubby places no one else wants to do! Unscrupulous bosses will pay you much less than they are compelled to by law! But then you too would be illegal so it shouldn't matter too much, should it? You'll be pleased that some of the people who will be adopting you at home and at work still retain some of the old traditions from back home—such as honour killing [stoning women, must, alas, be kept indoors]. Should you have any difficulty adjusting, then we can simply have you deported. Or better still, strap yourself to a DIY detonator and we'll pay for a one-way trip to London! Come over to the UK. The people are enlightened while the cold winds and seeping drizzle are good for your soul!*

In addition to those members of kitchen staff who had become frequent fliers on British Airways Fuselage Class, there were various locals (of brown as well as white skin) who tended the tables, serviced the bar and delivered the takeaways. A number of these concealed their supplementary earnings from the restaurant (wages were always paid in cash with no paper trail) from the relevant authorities. They were thus guilty of both benefit fraud and tax evasion. Occasionally, one or two would pop the odd amphetamine to help get through a slow evening's worth of chores (drug use is prevalent in dull inconsequential little Scottish towns) allowing them to set about their dreary routine with renewed vigour and heavily dilated pupils.

Overseeing operations would be the restaurant's owner—a man who had the uncanny ability for never allowing a Scotch glass to be empty no matter how much was consumed from it. From time to time, he was also partial to smoking a bit of heroin in the fire escape (merely smoking tobacco inside a public building is strictly forbidden in Scotland, let alone lighting up from tin foil). This did at least render him a more convivial albeit more incomprehensible individual. Until, that is, the time came to cough up the wages.

Bizarrely, the notion of actually having to pay somebody for their labour seemed morally repugnant to him. Especially when they requested something as obscene as the statutory minimum wage for the total number of hours they worked. Each week, a ridiculous parody of wage negotiation would ensue, with every minute of one's travails rigorously evaluated and scored. Patience would be stretched beyond the laws of physics by the endless haggling over petty cash. This petty cash, though, would mount up over the weeks, so if one relinquished so much as a quarter of an inch to Mr Shylock-Falstaff he would attempt to seize three thousand miles. Once, I had the temerity to ask for an extra hour's pay for an extra hour's exertion. The episode was subsequently used as a pretext to give part-time workers shorter shifts. This may have saved the owner enough to buy an extra bottle of *uisge beatha* a week, but resulted in all staff having to play catch-up all evening and thus deliver sub-standard service. Hardly surprising, then, that the bookings became fewer and the business became efficient only in the art of loss-making.

Another ingenious cost-cutting measure was to sack the best and most competent waiter and replace him with someone cheaper. Unfortunately, he was also a snotty incompetent lackey who earned his corn through spying on everyone else and reporting to the top.

Still, at the risk of maybe sounding a teensy bit schmaltzy or trite, I did (up to a point, it must be stressed) enjoy the camaraderie and solidarity which existed among us lumpen proletariat. There was something vaguely reassuring about being part of a multi-cultural community of minor lawbreakers. One thing to help maintain sanity—and one thing essential in almost every organisation—was juvenile internal rivalry. Echoing Europe's great opera houses, an 'us and them' mentality prevailed between cast (waiters, bar staff, delivery men, manager/host) and crew (cooks, delivery packer, dish washer, kitchen porter).

My designated role was to be in charge of the buffet. This was akin to being a goalkeeper in football: a great deal of prancing around for no purpose interspersed with moments of heightened frenzy, as one acted as the last line of defence between the customer and the product.

Incidentally, there was one occasion when the restaurant was actually blessed by the presence of an ex-international goalkeeper. Once a hero to millions, this former colossus between the sticks had regressed from prime athlete to dismal slob. He cut a sorrowful figure as years of notorious excess had taken their toll. His very appearance in a downmarket restaurant wearing downmarket clothes and sporting the bedraggled look of yesterday's man caused a few heads to turn and tongues to wag. He had ballooned in size, lost many teeth, while his wrinkled face drooped and sagged way beyond his years. When I handed him his plate and guided him through the buffet, he pointed to some decorative bottles of wine and semi-seriously blurted:

'I'll have those for starters.'

He nevertheless dined appreciatively and refrained from exhibiting any signs of his infamous boorishness. Mind you, he did chew with his mouth wide open and spoke while it was still full.

Anyway, back to somebody much more important: ME! My actual duties amounted to little more than having to act as a sort of petrol pump for human beings, but I did come across a wide assortment of anthropomorphic vehicles ranging from petite scooters to hefty juggernauts. And that was just the women.

When it came to the men, my lovely restaurant would have to transform from being a mere garage into a makeshift Valhalla while us waiters became Valkyries in order to cope with the demands of feasting Vikings following a hard stint of pillaging.

Indeed, the restaurant became a serai for a manner of tribes from the Dark Ages. We received our fair share of bohemians and goths (very nice people). The building was once attacked by vandals (not very nice people). There was the odd Frank (well, that was his name and he was odd—but in a nice way), and one night we entertained a pack of Huns. ('Huns' in local parlance refer to the hooligan element of supporters of Glasgow Rangers FC. These hooligans attack Roman Catholics and Roman Catholicism with the same brutality Attila and chums attacked the eternal city.) Arriving already drunk, these barbarians displayed great pride in showing one and all that their thinking had now progressed forward into the 17th century. A truly sickening night followed as they made merry by singing and chanting vile anti-Catholic sectarian songs and making mockery of the troubles in Northern Ireland.

As custodian of the buffet it was my responsibility to usher the barbarous, the civil, and the Barber of Seville (alas, Figaro never came) through their meal—from poppadoms and chutneys right through to coffee and mints. The buffet was 'all you can eat'. You'd be amazed by how much this could entail for some people. Think of a very large quantity of food. Quadruple it. Now say a prayer for the poor souls who had to tend the local sewage treatment plant.

Each week enough chickens to populate Botswana would have to be culled in order to placate the onrushing stampede of feral inbreds, some of whom would have been better off inside cages and have meat thrown at them. Long-dormant Hindu ethics were reignited within me, as the desire to avoid reincarnation as a chicken took hold. The prospect of spending a lifetime of forced feeding and forced multiple childbearing followed by a halal butchering and having one's dead arse covered in masala, deep fat-fried and passed through a kitchen of grease and grime on to the plate of some spotty Neanderthal who stinks to high heaven should be sufficient motivation to turn any carnivore into a devout veg.

Not all, however, shared my empathy towards domestic fowl, so it was my task to ensure that the grunting salivating hulks never held an empty platter in their sweaty palms. Meanwhile, their overworked hearts must have been beating frantically to circulate sluggish blood through massively clogged arteries. Perhaps they simply wished to accelerate their inevitable journey from the restaurant to the place behind it. Perhaps they were merely over-excited at the change of not having to eat a meal out of Styrofoam. Whatever the reason, the majority of customers were regulars who couldn't resist returning for more.

One can't quite figure out why. Of all the crimes and misdemeanours within the establishment, by far the most serious was the dishing up and serving of tripe to paying customers. Okay, they didn't pay over the top and left behind miserly tips (none of which staff were entitled to keep but looked to pocket at any given opportunity), while a great number displayed a staggering ignorance of food. (For instance, upon laying eyes on aubergines one woman exclaimed: 'Whit are dey big black "hings"?!') Their dinner could well have come spurting out of the ground through rusty pipes for all some of them cared.

In fairness, that's not too far off the truth. As someone of Indian origin I have become accustomed to Indian cuisine being served in my own home and in the home of a myriad of other people's homes I've visited in different parts of the globe. I spent two and-a-half years living and working in India and visited the land on numerous occasions prior. Never in all that time did I ever come across anything that was not bright orange. Nor one that didn't look like it had been soaked in the ink one finds in highlighter pens. Yet it was my job to cajole customers to lap up this gunk. It wasn't too strenuous, though. Like infants, diners were mesmerized by the crayon-hued nosh on display, made of a sickly combination of sugar and spice and all things not nice like artificial colourings, additives and preservatives containing every possible E-number known to scientists. Some were quite simple: a great deep layer of oil with minuscule chunks of meat, onion and veg desperately attempting to peep their tiny heads up to breathe—rather like unsuspecting coastal birds struck by an offshore oil slick.

Seasoned travellers, sophisticated urbanites and the assimilation of second-generation Indian culture into the mainstream have ensured that this desecration of non-Indian cuisine by dodgy non-Indians in dodgy non-Indian restaurants is being combated in the UK. Dull inconsequential little towns located at the back of beyond, thought to have slipped below the gastronomical radar at present. Ignorant diners with all the subtlety of a brontosaurus are continuously being suckered into slurping up such offal like pigs at a trough. One did not know whether to feel disgust or pity upon hearing cries like:

'Mmmm! This is fantastic! More please!'

All accompanied by a cacophony of belches and farts resounding like a mammoth orchestra composed solely of off-key bassoons. At least it did help to drown out the dreadful pop tunes playing on perpetual loop in the background.

Such terrible music did however go some way towards distracting customers away from some of the more shocking goings-on. Staff would pick food out with their sticky fingers in order to taste it, and dip fingers into food to test for temperature. A lot of food was dried, old leftovers simply reheated in the microwave. Dropped food and cutlery would be unhesitatingly picked up and placed back on to plates as if nothing had occurred. Each new batch of starters would be re-fried in the same vat of continuously re-used hydrogenated vegetable oil. Raw meat was sliced and chopped on the same boards as raw fruit and veg. Tables and countertops were wiped using dirty tablecloths. One could carry on recounting, but even Alexander Fleming's stomach might churn.

The whole time, the guzzlers were either oblivious to or uncaring of the various malpractices. I'm sure by now that many of them have done their vital organs irreparable damage or have sauntered on to an inescapable path towards coronary heart disease or something equally fatal.

As for me, I had the good sense to get out and exercise some more palatable options: abattoir attendant; dog food-taster; proctologist; bikini-waxer for elderly ladies; management consultancy; public relations; and human resources. I am no longer in contact with my former colleagues but hope that the better ones have had the good sense to get out and no longer wallow in slime. I still harbour all the pretences of a wannabe writer but mercifully no longer have to toil in such a grotesque environment for my pocket money.

Of course, cynics may point out that I parasitically obtained a fable from the whole experience—but let me add a cautionary moral with which Aesop would no doubt concur. For all those in similar shoes remember:

ONE MUST ALWAYS SUFFER FOR ONE'S ART!

The Sufi Way in Malerkotla

NIRUPAMA DUTT

I was out in the fields to gather fodder when Gaindarh Singh came running up to me, waving and shouting, 'Kanjara! You're making merry in the fields, you pimp, while over there in Sirhind our tenth Guru's sons are being bricked alive!'

I heard him and my heart sank. I stubbed out my beedi and we ran home. I asked my Bebe to pack us a few rotis and then we set off, Gaindarh and I, racing by the side of the canal. We reached Sirhind late in the evening—and do you know what we saw there? Thousands of people pouring in! The city was being swept and cleaned for a special durbar.

We spent the night somehow, our hearts pounding. The next morning the durbar assembled and the two Sahibzadas were brought there in chains. What can I tell you! The older one was a spitting image of our handsome Pappu, the landlord's son, who studies in the English school, and the younger one looked so like that tubby Gholu. The Sirhind-wala Nawab asked them to change their faith and then they would live. Even before the older one could speak, the younger Sahibzada thrust his chest out and said, 'Enough, Nawab! We will never change our faith!'

Puffing with rage, his face red as blood, the nawab ordered that the two children be bricked alive.

At this the Malerkotle-wala Nawab got up and raised his voice: 'This is unjust!'

I too got up, raised my arm and cried out, 'It is absolutely unjust!'

This is how the famed Mast, the lead comic actor of a left-wing theatre group of Barnala, told a story. A remnant of the *Mirasi-Bhand* tradition of feudal Punjab, he pulled large crowds at Communist rallies in the '60s. His art lay in the fact that he gave first-person narrations of historical events, improvising to make himself and his audience characters in the times he was enacting. Politicians in Punjab still hire comedy stars like Navjot Singh Sidhu and Bhagwant Maan for their rallies, but old-timers say that none can match the standards set by the unlettered Mast, who retained in his heart hundreds of tales and told them with as much passion as humour. The moving story of the Sahibzadas was a favourite. Time would stand suspended as his listeners watched and listened, becoming part of their history.

Time indeed stood suspended as I made a journey to Malerkotla town in the Malwa region of Punjab, where the story of the Sahibzadas is as alive today as it was some 300 years ago. Over the centuries, Malerkotla has earned a unique reputation as an oasis of calm in conflict-torn Punjab. Muslims, Sikhs and Hindus have lived here without a single act of violence during the holocaust of Partition and the dark days of militancy. It is the spirit, people say, of the Sufis, and the nawab who stood up for justice.

*

I take an afternoon bus from Chandigarh, hoping for the best. My only contact in Malerkotla is Azad Siddiqui, a budding politician of Akali Dal (Badal) whom I've never met. I do know another person there, but I'm reluctant to contact him. He is a namesake of the legendary playback singer of Hindi films.

Malerkotle-wala Mohammad Rafi is a lecturer of Urdu in the local Government College—also a maverick painter, orator and theatre-person, and a man who can derail all your plans with endless talk. The last time I travelled to Malerkotla, some four years ago, the entire trip had been hijacked twice: first by my poet-friend Manjit Tiwana, and then by Mr Rafi.

Manjit, instead of taking me directly to Malerkotla, had driven me miles away in the opposite direction, towards a sacred grove. We would soon be at the *dera* of Baba Marhu Das, she said. 'My mother would go to him, holding my hand, to ask for the boon of a son. I was the fifth daughter and my mother had to suffer many tortures for not bearing a son...' When we reached Marhu Das di Gufa, it became clear to me that Manjit had imagined all the treks with her mother to the Baba's cave. Marhu Das had died long before the mother was born. When we finally arrived at my intended destination, Manjit took me to a complimentary dinner with Rafi at Coronet Restaurant, which is part of his family business. In exchange, we became his captive viewers and were shown painting after painting from among the hundreds he had made, listening to him talk about them till late into the night. Shortly after that meeting Rafi gave an interview to a regional daily and went on record saying that he was the richest man in Punjab because he had so much art. The story appeared with the headline 'Richest Man in Punjab', and the Income-Tax Department conducted a raid at his home. All they found were mountains of canvases that he himself had painted, and closed the file.

These days, I hear, Rafi heads the new Urdu Akademi in Malerkotla. I will meet him only at the end of the trip: risking a meeting at the beginning may mean putting off my book by a few more years—and I've had quite enough of my wayward nature. Years ago, after I brought my first love story to its unhappy conclusion, I decided that it was 'novel' material. I had barely written some fifty pages when the second real-life romance began... and so on. This became a pattern. The dilemma always was whether to write of the past love or to live the next one. Now, with the storms of youth behind me, I could do without distractions and actually finish the book I'd promised to write on Punjab, perhaps my only enduring love.

It takes me close to an hour to begin my journey out of Chandigarh. There is no direct bus to Malerkotla, and the connecting one to Morinda is reluctant to leave the terminal. It is full, with a whole lot of people standing, and arguments have erupted between passengers with seat numbers and those without. One wise sardar tries to quash it all by saying, 'We are not going to Canada. Morinda is just an hour away, what do we need seat numbers for?' The driver, at least, sees the sense in this and starts the bus. We reach Morinda early enough and I catch a bright red semi-deluxe bus to Malerkotla. The pictures and motifs decorating the front of the bus spell pluralism with a capital P. Framed paintings of Guru Nanak and Guru Gobind Singh, the first Guru and the tenth, have pride of place. Then there are paintings of some saints and mendicants: Sai Baba, Kabir, Sant Kirpal Singh. Bhagat Singh appears in a calendar-art portrait on the toolbox, donning his famous hat and with two peacocks flanking him on either side. In the left corner are etchings of the Cross, the Om and Ik-Onkar. Pasted at the bottom of the glass partition between the driver and the passengers is a picture of Punjab's first and greatest Sufi poet, Sheikh Farid. And above him, a much bigger picture of the Sahibzadas, two cherubic boys in the court of the stone-hearted nawab of Sirhind.

The TV in the bus is beaming a comedy show. Chacha, the anchor, cracks jokes mostly at the cost of the second sex and the accompanying starlet makes funny faces but does not laugh. Now Chacha is taking a dig at women drivers. To prove his point, he conjures a sleek little red car and a life-size cutout of Sonia Gandhi. 'Sonia Gandhi knew she could never drive this country, so she put Sardar Manmohan Singh on the driver's seat!' At this, a small cutout of a mousy Manmohan Singh pops up on the front seat and the laughter of the passengers mixes with the taped guffaws.

That the country now has a Sikh Prime Minister, that a bus can carry Sikh, Hindu and Muslim religious symbols side by side and people can travel without fear is enough to make you forget how much violence Punjab has suffered. Just as, during the darkest days of Partition, of militancy and state crackdown in the 1980s, it was easy to forget that Sikh history also has a strong tradition of communal harmony and humanism. There is no place where this is most apparent than in Malerkotla, where Muslims—who comprise roughly seventy per cent of the population—Hindus and Sikhs have lived in peace for centuries.

The most celebrated event in the town's history dates back over 300 years. Guru Gobind Singh, the founder of the Khalsa, had earned the wrath of Mughal officials who saw him and his creed as a threat to their empire. Constant harassment and persecution forced the Guru and his closest followers to finally leave Anandpur, the seat of the Khalsa, on the night of 5 December 1704. During the long trek, the Guru's two youngest sons, nine-year-old Sahibzada Zorawar Singh and six-year-old Sahibzada Fateh Singh, and his mother, Mata Gujri, were separated from him. Their own cook betrayed them and the three were captured and taken to Sirhind. Nawab Wazir Khan, the Mughal governor of Sirhind, ordered them walled alive unless they embraced Islam. The Guru's sons would not accept conversion and the worst happened on the morning of 27 December 1704. The only protest against such a fate for the innocent boys had come from Nawab Sher Mohammad Khan of Malerkotla. The letter he wrote to Aurangzeb in Delhi is still in the proud possession of his heirs. Sher Mohammad wrote: 'The Governor of Sirhind province, with a view to avenging the disobedience of the Guru... has without any fault or crime of the guiltless and innocent children, simply on the basis of their being the scions of Guru Gobind Singh, condemned them to execution and has proposed to wall them up till they die... This action appears to me to be absolutely against the dictates of Islam and the laws propounded by the founder of Islam (May Allah's blessings be showered upon Him). Your Majesty's servant is afraid that the enactment of such an atrocity will be an ugly blot on the face of Your Majesty's renowned justice and righteousness...'

Neither Wazir Khan nor Aurangzeb heeded this voice of sanity. When news of the tragedy reached the Guru, he was weeding grass at Talwandi Sabu, where he had taken refuge. His first reaction, they say, was to announce that he would tear out the roots of his adversaries. Then he asked, 'Did no one cry out in protest?' When informed of the lone resistance of the nawab of Malerkotla, the Guru said, 'His roots will forever be green.'

The bus passes the picturesque gurdwara at Fatehgarh Sahib, where the Sahibzadas met their end. Retribution came when Banda Bahadur, a disciple of the tenth Guru at Nanded in Maharashtra, rode across half the country and razed the fort of

Sirhind and killed Wazir Khan. A memorial was built at Fatehgarh to the two Sahibzadas and their grandmother (who died of shock shortly after her grandsons were bricked alive). In 1746, Maharaja Karam Singh of Patiala built Gurdwara Fatehgarh on the site. The eastern gate of the gurdwara was dedicated to the memory of the nawab of Malerkotla.

I have been to Fatehgarh several times before, but for other reasons. The district of Fatehgarh Sahib along with Kurukshetra in Haryana and Kangra in Himachal forms the triangle of religious districts where the female to male sex ratio is the lowest in the country. This, too, is Punjab.

*

We are moving into Sirhind, when the conductor informs me that I should get off at Khanna and take another bus, since the one we are on will now by-pass Malerkotla and head straight for Ludhiana. It is a while before a bus for Malerkotla arrives. There are very few passengers and I get a seat all to myself. The drive is beautiful. The narrow road is nearly traffic-free and lined on both sides with *shisham* and *kikar* trees. The orange ball of the setting sun accompanies the bus, almost right through, suspended above a fine picture of pastoral Punjab. My eyes are soothed.

But my heart is uneasy. It is getting late and there is no way I can return to Patiala to spend the night at Manjit's, as I had planned. Where will I stay? I really should have got in touch with Deepak before starting. Deepak, the nawab of my erstwhile love life. For me many towns, villages and journeys have an emotional quotient all in the wrong measure. Anyway, the lost Deepak connection might just be some use… Just then, my friend Vijaya calls—'As soon as you reach, call Azad and he will come and pick you up.'

It is dark when Azad comes to fetch me at the bus stand. He is younger than I'd imagined, and quite affable, although a little disappointed that I have not brought Rani Balbir Kaur's telephone number with me. He's a great fan of the Chandigarh-based theatre star. He drives me straight to the rancid-smelling restaurant of a rundown hotel, where we settle down for an excellent meal of dal makhani, mixed vegetables and hot tandoori rotis. 'I was hoping you'd bring me Rani Balbir Kaur's number,' Azad complains, but pleasantly enough. 'Now that our Badal Akali Dal has come to power, we want to make her a chairperson of one of the corporations or foundations. Something befitting her talent and stature.' Young Azad is the general secretary of the party for Sangrur district. 'The seat here has gone to Razia Sultan of the Congress again, but at least our party will form the ministry in Chandigarh, thanks to the BJP.'

I tell Azad that I'm happy to stay at this hotel, but he will have none of it. He has decided to take charge of my life. He takes me to another, recently built hotel called Maharaja Palace. The room is passable and the attached bathroom clean. Azad likes it more than I do and parks himself in one of the two ornate chairs by the bed. He has asked a member of Malerkotla's famous Sherwani family to visit us and tell me all about the Sufi tradition of the town. The Sherwani heir is late in coming, so Azad narrates his own hard-luck-to-success story, at one time the quintessential Punjabi story of resilience, hard work and pride, before immigration became the dream narrative. 'I am the eldest of six children,' Azad says. 'My father was a poor man, he repaired bags. He educated me up to Class X and then I set up my own shop and worked hard repairing bags. Now I have two shops, a school and I head a number of NGOs. I did my Plus II privately. My brothers run the business now and I have time to be in politics.' He has fixed the marriage of one of his sisters recently and is planning to marry an educated Muslim girl himself, someone who will help him in his politics and business.

Then it is his turn to question me. When in Punjab, you should be prepared for all kinds of invasions, including of your privacy. It is one big village where everyone should know everything about the other and especially about a woman who travels alone and is not afraid of staying in a hotel all by herself. He wants to know my age. I tell him that it is a complete pack of cards minus the jokers and he exclaims, 'But you don't look it! You look only thirty-five!' I'm quite sure this remark isn't meant to be taken seriously, yet it more than makes up for the tiring journey and his inquisitiveness. Then he wants to know why I am not married and somehow it slips that the man I wanted to marry would not marry me. 'Oh! So you are the victim of a failed love affair!' he says brightly. 'Just so!' I reply, and now I am no longer a mystery to him and before I know it he has offered to stay the night with me in the hotel. Amazed, I wonder what he wants but it is only his small-town politeness, for he soon adds, 'I want that you should not be inconvenienced in any way.' 'No, no, you shouldn't worry,' I say. 'I am used to staying alone and I quite like it.' He frowns.

At last the fifteenth-generation Shehzada of the Sherwani family arrives with his family tree and photocopies of documents relevant to the history of Malerkotla. Shehzada Ajmal Khan Ajmal Sherwani is an earnest young man in his mid-thirties and lives off the legacy of agri farms and stud farms. He writes poetry and has just returned after reading his verses at a poetry symposium in Jalandhar. There he recited verses in the secular tradition of his hometown. He recites one for me: *Mera watan, ke hai phoolon ka ek guldasta/ Ham ise pyar ke guldaan mein sajaenge* (My country is a bouquet of flowers and we will adorn it in the vase of love). Not memorable poetry, but at least the thought is as noble as his ancestry.

*

With Shehzada as the narrator, we go back some 600 years to understand the history of this unique town. Malerkotla is one of the oldest states in Punjab. It came up almost a hundred years before Babur established Mughal rule in India. History authenticates that a Sherwani Afghan of Daraban, Sheikh Saddaruddin Sardar-I-Jahan, was spiritually inclined from his boyhood. In 1449, he reached Multan and became the disciple of Pir Bahawal Shah. When the Pir was sure that his disciple was well versed in spirituality, he asked him to go out and help humanity. Sheikh Saddaruddin chose a raised mound near the old village of Maler to build his hut, and there he spent his time in prayer.

One night, Bahlol Lodhi camped at Maler on his way to conquer Delhi. It was a stormy night and the only lamp aflame was in the hut on the mound. Bahlol went to meet the man whose lamp the harsh winds could not extinguish. Sheikh Saddaruddin, whom we know today as Hazrat Sheikh, welcomed Bahlol into his hut and prophesied that Delhi would indeed be his. When Bahlol accomplished his mission, he returned to thank this man of God. The thanksgiving included marriage to his daughter Taj Murassa and a gift of Maler and the surrounding villages and three lakh rupees in dowry. This was in 1454.

Some years later the Sheikh married again, this time Murtaza 'Rajan', daughter of Rai Behram, a ruler of Kapurthala. Interestingly, Sheikh Saddaruddin bequeathed the Sufi tradition to the lineage from his first wife and the dominion to the lineage from his second. Showing me a detailed chart of the genealogy, Shehzada says, 'I belong to the line that inherited the Sufi tradition. I know it all. Journalists come here and meet all the wrong people. They go back and quote rickshaw-wallahs and chai-wallahs. What would *they* know?' I think of asking the young Shehzada if he's sure he has inherited the Sufi heritage and not the dominion after all, but then let it be.

A grandson of Hazrat Sheikh founded the province of Malerkotla, the Shehzada goes on. His name was Mohammad Bayazid Khan. He saved the life of Emperor Aurangzeb from an approaching tiger and rose to a high rank in the Mughal court. He got recognition as an independent ruler and was granted the right to build a defensive wall and a fort and thus *kotla* (fort) was added to the original name, Maler. In keeping with the sufi traditions of his family, Bayazid Khan asked a Sufi saint, Shah Fazl Chishti, and a Hindu sadhu, Damodar Das, to lay the foundation stone. As the old folks say, because the foundation was secular, religious tolerance came to be the key word, and as long as the fort wall stands, there can be no communal discord here.

The last nawab of Malerkotla, Iftikhar Ali Khan, in spite of his four wives, died childless at the age of seventy-eight in 1982. While his first three wives were of nawabi descent, his fourth wife Sajida Begum was a local Punjabi Pathan girl. She was big, bold and beautiful and after the nawab died she took a couple of more husbands. She was also linked with Giani Zail Singh, the former President, who came to visit her many times. Rumours abounded. The satirist Gurnam Singh Tir even wrote a popular mock-ballad, a la *Heer-Ranjha*, about the two. Our Shehzada, however, is keen to make saints of the dead. 'You know, Sajida Begum was considered a sister by Gianiji. He came to meet her every year so she could tie a *rakhi* on him,' he says.

Gianiji—like the Akali leader Surjit Singh Barnala—also had a special place in his heart for Master Jivana, a celebrated tailor of the town, and would get all his coats and sherwanis stitched by him. The best tailors, as someone said to me, will be found in the gentlest, most laidback places where leisure is given its due. The laidback nature of the Malerkotla *riyasat* is evident from the fact that the last nawab refused a pre-Independence proposal to upgrade the railway station to a junction so that the people would not be disturbed at night. The junction came up instead at nearby Dhuri town.

*

My hosts leave for the night, wishing me *shabba khair*. A smattering of Urdu words in the Punjabi of Malerkotla makes their language far sweeter than that in other parts of Malwa. Alone, I pull the gold-and-brown tiger-stripe quilt over myself. But sleep is elsewhere, and I get into communion with Malerkotla's ghosts and my own. Memories rise and glide right through the survivor's armour of forgetfulness. I think of my childhood in Chandigarh. Silence was the lot of children born in the decade after Partition. Parents did not wish to pass the madness and horror to their children. I had never seen a Muslim till my mother took me with her to Pakistan, to visit her sister who had stayed on. I was surprised to see apparitions draped in black. I pointed to one and asked my mother, 'What is this?' She laughed and replied, 'This is a lady!'

I was to see many such ladies, bearded men, young boys in skull caps and Muslims who spoke Punjabi in Pakistan. But through childhood I continued to believe that there were no Punjabi Muslims in India. Perhaps because the elders always said, 'They all went to Pakistan.' Years later, I learnt that while a few million had indeed migrated, thousands of others had been butchered, even in the villages that were grouped to form the city of Chandigarh. Many of those who stayed on had to take Hindu and Sikh identities. In Manimajra, a village of Chandigarh, several Muslims returned to their original names only some fifty years after Partition. Recently, I shared these thoughts while reading a paper on Partition literature in Lahore, and theatre activist Madeeha Gauhar responded that she could identify with what I said. She too had grown up thinking that there were no Punjabi Hindus in Lahore.

*

Deeper into the night, still sleepless, I think of Deepak. His village, Mubarakpur Chungan, is just seven kilometres from Malerkotla. I should have called him before coming here, but I'd hesitated because the last time he called me, some years ago, I had cursed him and banged the telephone down. On an impulse, now, I dial his number. His sleepy voice answers and then I hear the receiver being slammed back. I chuckle, thinking that it is fortunate we did not marry after all. Clearly, our body clocks did not match.

The singing mobile wakes me early the next morning. It is Deepak, and when he learns that I am in Malerkotla, he is most offended that I didn't take his help. 'What a beautiful city and what culture!' he exclaims. 'Rehmat qawwal would cast a spell with his *Sufiana qalam*. Anno Jaan and Zarina Jaan were the two most famous and sought after *tawaif*s of the town…' I listen to him go on excitedly about the Sufis and qawwals and dancing girls of Malerkotla and wonder if I'd only imagined him hanging up on me last night.

'You know, while I was studying there, a tall young man with film-hero looks would come to play hockey in the college grounds. He was a tubewell mechanic. His clothes were very colourful and we would laugh at him. Later he went to Bombay and became the famous film star Dharmendra. The photographs he sent for the 1958 *Filmfare* talent hunt contest were taken at John's Studio in Sadar Bazaar. Some years ago when I went to Bombay to invite him for a World Punjabi Conference and told him I was from Malerkotla district, he wouldn't let me leave and kept talking of the old times for two hours. I could understand— there was something magical about Malerkotla when we were growing up. I still roam in my dreams in the lost grandeur of Moti Bazaar… Have you been there yet?'

Later that morning I visit the various heritage monuments the city boasts, but it is heritage going to seed. Most well tended is the spacious Idgah, which the residents of the town say is the best in Asia. The famed Sheesh Mahal, which was the home of Sajida Begum, is in shambles. After the death of the begum many claimants turned up and the government was forced to seal it, pending the dispute being settled, which may take decades. The glory of the Purana Mahal is lost. Much of its land and outhouses have been sold and new colonies of match-box apartments surround it. Many no longer call it the palace. They call it Tonk-wala Bangla, for it is now little more than a bungalow. In this palace of yore lives the frail and ailing but still beautiful Tonk-wali Begum, one of the four begums of the last nawab.

Tonk was a princely state of Rajasthan given to Amir Khan, a freebooter of Afghan descent and a Pindari leader, after he submitted to the British during the 1817 Pindari wars. Nawab Iftikhar Ali Khan's initial connection with Tonk was hunting, his great passion. His hunting trips would take him away from Malerkotla for long periods, to Kandaghat in Himachal Pradesh and to Tonk. On one of his hunting expeditions he lost his heart to Munawar-u-nissa, the comely princess of Tonk, and took her as his second wife. Mohammad Mehmood, who along with his family is in the service of the begum, says: 'My father served her and now my family and I look after her. Nawab Sahib spent the longest part of his life with her. They also had a baby girl but she passed away when she was but six days old. I have seen the begum since my childhood and she is the kindest person in the world.' The sword and the *hukamnama* of gratitude gifted to Nawab Sher Mohammad Khan by Guru Gobind Singh are in her possession. Much else is lost, but the begum lives with dignity in the evening of her life.

Moti Bazaar and Laal Bazaar, built on the designs of the bazaars of Jaipur, are being eclipsed by crude contemporary construction. Only a few of the old shops with carved balconies still remain as slender proof of the old grandeur. Every second shop is an embroidery shop now, because the town has a flourishing cottage industry embroidering army and police badges. All over the bazaar I see election posters of the recently elected Razia Sultan flanked by Punjab Congress leader Rajinder Kaur Bhattal and the 'Maharani' of Patiala, Parneet Kaur. Razia is a local Gujjar girl, acclaimed for her beauty, who worked with Sajida Begum in her younger days and is now married to a senior Punjab police officer. To my joy, I discover John's Studio in Sadar Bazaar. Its owner who had clicked Dharam Bhaji's pictures is no more but his son still runs the studio.

The *mazaar* of Sheikh Hazrat at the entrance to the bazaars in old Maler is a shocking sight in a town that prides itself on its Sufi heritage. Someone had thought of renovating it but had clearly given up long ago, and there is a great mess of refuse and building material. Families of the old Afghans still live around the mazaar, clearly oblivious to its slow ruin.

'The local Muslims respect the saint but do not believe in him because they are Islamic,' says left-wing Punjabi writer S. Tarsem. He has taught a lifetime in a local college and knows the town like the back of his hand. 'However, the mazaar has a great following among Hindus and Sikhs all the way from Barnala to Bathinda. They come in hundreds all year round and in thousands at the time of the Urs.' I'm ambivalent about the faith of these thousands who come to the mazaar. I know that a large majority come to seek the saint's blessings for a male child. Some years ago this had led to a strange phenomenon: Kade-wala Baba. He set up shop behind the Idgah and gave couples iron kadas that would guarantee a male child. His fame spread, and people from all over the country started coming to him for the kada in exchange for generous offerings in cash and kind. The one train that passed the town began to halt at his *dera*. It is said he distributed a lakh and twenty-five thousand bangles before some wise men of the town drove him away (the cynical maintain that they were provoked to act because the savvy sadhu's growing fame meant that less and less people came to Sheikh Hazrat's mazaar).

*

Sitting with Tarsem at his home I ask him if there has indeed never been a single case of religious violence in his town. He replies that I could wait another 100 years if that was what I wanted to see and I would still be disappointed. There's something in the air of Malerkotla, he says, something in its soil that changes men of hate. 'In those days of '46-'47, people were being killed just two yards outside our territory, but anyone who entered, Hindu, Sikh or Muslim, was miraculously saved. There was no violence here even after the felling of the Babri Masjid in '92, even though nearly seventy per cent of the population is Muslim. The people here are peace-loving and if ever there is any attempt by any mischievous forces it is suppressed well in time.' Sardar Balwant Singh, who was the minister of law and order in Malerkotla during Partition, records in his account of the times: 'About one lakh Muslims from other parts of Punjab took shelter here. Not a single killing took place... All the Muslims who converged at Malerkotla were safely sent to Pakistan with the assistance of Sardar Patel. A battalion of the army was sent to help the migrants across.'

Deepak tells me later that he went with the other boys of his village to Dhuri, ten kilometres away, to see what was absent in

Malerkotla—killing and looting. 'Wells were choked with bodies and Muslim homes were being looted. I saw a bull in one home. I liked it, so I brought it back to my village.' Once a looter always a looter, I say and have the last laugh.

The visit to Tarsem's house proves to be a turning point in the unfolding of the Malerkotla mystique. He gives me a short story titled 'Nath' written by Chandigarh-based writer Mohan Bhandari. Another gift is the novella *Anup Kaur* by late Harnam Das Sehrai who wrote scores of novels in Punjabi, all based on Sikh history. Bhandari's story is a quasi-fictional account of the unhappy lives of the glittering courtesans of Malerkotla. Bhandari writes: 'I visited Anno Jaan's kotha once with my friend Shauqat, to see the new *kabootri* who had been brought there. Shauqat and the young girl lost their hearts to each other. Of course, they could never come together because a man old enough to be her father removed her *nath* (nose-ring) and deflowered her... When we resurrect feudal times, we must not forget the ugliness.'

For me the dilemma comes with *Anup Kaur*, and puts me in a predicament too, as I chronicle the history of this principality. But that happens later, when I read the novel at night. That evening, I am still trying to contact the missing Azad who had promised to take me to meet the surviving heirs of the famed Mirasi performing tradition. When I finally get him on the phone, he says, 'I will bring everyone to the hotel.' I try to reason that my going to meet them would be a better idea; I'd like to see them in their environment. There's a stony silence at the other end. There goes my chance to visit old Maler at night where, Azad has told me, stalls of tea, paan-beedi, sweets and frothy milk that they call *doodh-malai* remain open till the wee hours. I could have done with a nice hot tumbler of frothy milk after the rounds of the day. Maybe I can ask him to take me out after we've met the Mirasis.

Azad comes late in the evening with two strapping young men for me to interview. They are local bodybuilders! The older of the two is a dark and stocky trainer called Mohammad Sharif Boss and the other hulk, Mumtaz Ahmad Tony, has the startling good looks of Dharmendra. He has also been Mr Punjab. What follows is a treatise on physical fitness, bodybuilding and the powerful Punjabi physique. Boss tells me that once at the Lal Qila in Delhi a police officer stopped the two of them and asked, 'Are you from Punjab? You can't be locals, we see only ill-fed *chhachhunders* here.' Tony adds, 'Bodybuilders don't have to introduce themselves. Their bodies tell the tale.' Together they run the local Great Sports and Welfare Club and help young men give up alcohol, drugs and tobacco. Besides, they are proud advertisements of Punjabi health and well-being, and get paid for that.

Happily, Sardar Ali of the Mirasi village of Matoi arrives and the conversation shifts from the body to the soul. Sardar belongs to the lineage of Ustad Chanan Shah, his grandfather, and Ustad Abdul Majid Khan, his father. He talks reverentially of the late Ustad Barqat Husain of the Patiala Gharana who lived here, and the late Rehmat Qawwal. Barqat Husain's wife Salma was famous in her own right as a ghazal singer, but she too is dead, and I lose my chance of meeting a woman of substance; the entire milieu is oppressively masculine here. Sardar says disapprovingly, 'Ustad Sahib should not have married her. She was raised in the *tawaif* tradition. However, he lost his heart to her when he had gone to Uttar Pradesh for a concert. He was very young then.' Sardar, very young himself, but utterly sure of

41

his heart, is an ambitious fellow. He tells me he will soon establish the Abdul Majid Institute of Music and Art, named after his father. The conversation meanders to this and that, and somehow the young men start reciting a few couplets of Urdu for my benefit in their pronounced Punjabi accent. I have said earlier that the smattering of Urdu sweetens the Punjabi spoken in Malerkotla. But the Punjabi *lehaza* does nothing for the Urdu they speak.

Shero-o-shairi over, the moral gang of four robs me of my tumbler of frothy milk at old Maler—I can't be part of their night out. 'We cannot take you there,' Azad says decisively. 'It is not proper. This is a Muslim town and women stay in purdah.' This is the end. Angry words gather at the tip of my tongue. He'll never have Rani Balbir Kaur's telephone number; at least not from me. I remain in my zenana of Maharaja Palace, sipping bland chicken soup and wishing myself in Lahore, where I would be one among many women without purdah, enjoying the fare at Food Street on Nisbat Road past midnight. In fact, right now I wouldn't even mind reclining at Mocha Café in Chandigarh, having my masala tea and able to think kindly of Punjab.

This is the mood I take to my reading of *Anup Kaur* that night. While the stories of the Sahibzadas, the Nawab and Hazrat Sheikh are well known, I have never heard any mention of Anup Kaur in all that I have been told about Malerkotla. But women have strange ways of reaching out and this young woman smuggles herself into my *khwabgah*, my refuge of dreams, in a slim novella. She completes my journey. The novella, written like a lascivious pamphlet, tells the story of the resistance of a beautiful young girl called Anup Kaur, an expert warrior and a friend of the Sahibzadas. Abducted by Nawab Sher Mohammad Khan, the same man who stood up courageously to defend the Sahibzadas, she chose to thrust a dagger into her breast rather than change her faith and marry him. The novella says that Anup's soul haunts the palace of the nawab and does not allow him a wink of sleep even in death, as she didn't all the years that he was alive. I don't know how the nawab coped, but my sleep is gone.

The ghost of the unborn, unfulfilled, oppressed womanhood is to chase me all through my journey in Punjab. For the moment, I dismiss Anup's story, the blot on the celebrated nawab's reputation. This is all fiction, I tell myself. Later, though, I find references to this girl in several Sikh texts and in the writings of historian Ganda Singh. The historian says that when Banda Bahadur came to avenge the murder of the Sahibzadas, he razed Sirhind to the ground but did not destroy Malerkotla because of that one cry of protest by the nawab. However, he exhumed the body of Anup, cremated it according to Sikh rites, and set her soul to rest. Few people remember her; no one rose in her defence.

The following morning, Azad asks me to stop by his school, and there he introduces me to the young Hindu and Muslim teachers. As we talk, the subject of purdah comes up. Not all the teachers support the practice. Azad intervenes to pronounce: 'Women must remain in purdah. That is the right thing for them. No boy will ever harass a girl wearing a burqa.'

On my way out of the town, I spot a small crowd at the mazaar of Hazrat Sheikh. Men and women praying for a male child—and does the saint grant their wish each time? Is Anup Kaur's soul really at rest?

Yet, the legend of Malerkotla lives on. Perhaps it is not for individuals to judge. Human existence is never without its flaws; even one act of kindness, however small, is a gift to be grateful for. In the crowded bus that takes the route from Amargarh and Nabha to reach Patiala, I look back with love at Malerkotla that still shows hope for humanity, never mind its failings. There is some charm in the remnants of decadent Nawabi honour. I can't deny the fondness I feel for the righteous Azad, the bodybuilders, the sanctimonious Mirasi singer and the fifteenth-generation Shehzada who might one day learn to love the rickshaw-wallahs and chai-wallahs. Kind thoughts fly to Tarsem, Rafi-ul-art and that damned Deepak, too. The turmoil of the night is over and calm is settling in as I journey back home. Does it have something to do with the Sufi way in Malerkotla? The rough rustic song playing in the bus wants to know: *Kehde yaar di jalebi khaadi, Hunn bada mittha boldi* (Which lover's fed you a jalebi that you speak so sweetly now)? All right, I'll send Azad Rani's number after all. And I think I will be back for that tumbler of milk in old Maler. And a jalebi to sweeten my tongue.

One Day in DC

ASHOK MALIK

Yes, got it! It took some searching and rummaging amid a mess of papers on a spectacularly untidy desk but I finally found it. It's fairly nondescript really, only a tattered, creased piece of paper saying 'Taxi Cab Receipt', with the following name and address scribbled on the reverse:

Solomon Negussie
4506 Maxfield Dr
Annandale VA
220003

To me, it's obviously more than just a taxi receipt, which is why I'm burdening you with this story. It's a remembrance of the strangest taxi ride I've ever had. It's a promise, alas, yet unfulfilled. In retrospect—lovely word that: it allows you to sit back, intellectualize everything that's ever happened, and pretend you knew its import all along—it's also a lesson in diplomacy and soft power.

Of course I knew none of this when the piece of paper was hurriedly thrust into my palm, as I got out of a taxi on Washington DC's K Street for my final appointment after a two-and-a-half day whirlwind visit to the power capital of the world.

I had spent the morning, as I had the previous two days, rushing from one think-tank to the next, one thought-shop to its neighbour, doing two appointments at the State Department in one afternoon, and scurrying to make it to a briefing at the other end of town in-between, seemingly always late, trying to keep up with impossible American standards of punctuality and time ('I have a meeting at 1.30 that is a seven-minute walk from my office, so I can give you twenty minutes from 1.00. I will have to leave at 1.20 or, at the latest, 1.22, so please don't be late'), I was physically exhausted, mentally fatigued.

It can be overwhelming, DC can. This is a place teeming with more strategic thinkers and foreign policy analysts per square inch than the lunch room at Delhi's India International on a midweek afternoon in November. In my time in the city I'd met think-tank specialists, strategic affairs boffins, and diplomatic veterans who'd told me Central Asia was the key to a stable Afghanistan, and Pakistan was a part of the problem; Central Asia was the key to a stable Afghanistan and Pakistan was a part of the solution; India should get involved in Central Asia; India should get involved in West Asia; India would inevitably look to East Asia; actually, it was in India's interest to nurture an open-border South Asia; the nuclear deal was a done deal; the nuclear deal was not a done deal; Musharraf was a neo-con man; Musharraf was only a con man; the Bush foreign policy goals would not be reversed by a future administration; of course, the Bush foreign policy goals would be dumped by a future administration; India's place at the high table was a given; India's place at the high table was a work in progress. India's place at the high table? Which place? What high table?

Every opinion was backed up by a singular confidence and certitude. At each meeting, I was handed a sheaf of documents, policy papers, briefing papers, abstracts of PhD theses, summaries of book projects. Everybody seemed to know somebody who knew somebody in the previous (Bill) Clinton administration, the upcoming (Hillary) Clinton administration, the Reagan administration, the (elder) Bush administration, the (younger) Bush administration, the whatever administration.

Far more than Delhi, I realized, Washington is an insular little village. It lives in a universe of its own and the rest of the United States—and, doubtless, the rest of the world—is an occupational irritant, occasionally needed to test your theories on.

Anyhow, Simple Simon was in town and it was his—mine—third morning in the District of Columbia. I had a train to catch in the afternoon, luggage to pick up from the hotel right before that, and one last meeting to finish. I had planned to walk to K Street but a combination of delayed departure from my previous interlocutor's office room, a strengthening drizzle, and taking a wrong turn, decided otherwise; in Washington, one wrong turn is usually all it takes to destroy your day: Bush went to Iraq; mercifully, I only hailed a taxi.

I jumped in panting, excited and patently frazzled. The taxi man was calm and unperturbed, as only taxi men can be, as if half expecting me to point ahead and exclaim, 'Chase that car!'

Real life is more ordinary. 'Are you okay?' he asked, and the conversation began.

'Yes, it's my last day before I go home, and I've been running late all morning.'

'Where is home?'

'Far away—India...'

'Ah, India...'

We lapsed into silence. I presumed *he* had been silenced by the mention of India, too distant and too remote to touch his life and consciousness, making it hard for him to add to the banter.

I was so very wrong. He sprung it on me, almost by stealth: 'I had Indian teachers in school.'

'Really? And where was school?'

'Ethiopia. Addis Ababa.'

'You're Ethiopian?'

'Yup, came to the United States twenty years ago.'

'So you had Indian teachers... which subjects?'

'Oh, all of them. Science, mathematics, geography. All of them had Indian teachers. Mrs Kurien taught me English. Do you know her?"

'Er, actually no... Did you stay in touch?'

'No. I left soon after.'

Again, he went quiet, and I proceeded to stare out of the window, thinking of questions I would ask my final interviewee and, before that, what excuses I would conjure up for being ten minutes late, and how I would get on that train to New York and, eventually, fly home.

The Abyssinian at the wheel hadn't finished. As we turned into K Street, his voice quickened, betraying a certain nervousness and, even if I couldn't grasp it immediately, emotion. 'Have you seen *Mother India*?' he asked

'*Mother India*, the film? Nargis? Of course, half a dozen times.'

'Yes, yes, Na Giss, Na Giss! It was a very moving film. I saw it many times in Ethiopia.'

'You saw *Mother India* in Ethiopia, interesting. Did you see other Indian films as well? Raj Kapoor? *Awaara*?'

'I don't remember, only *Mother India*, I remember. It was a very moving film. It always made me cry.'

'Actually, it makes me cry too, but I always thought *Mother India* could only make an Indian cry... Strange and nice hearing this from you.'

'But, you know, Indians in Washington and in Annandale, where I live, are different. They're... different.'

'Why?'

'I've been trying to find a CD or DVD of *Mother India* to see it again, to show it to my children. I want to share it with them. But your Indians shops don't have it. Every time I go they tell me "No *Mother India*, nobody watches such an old film. Take new films, more fun, more songs." But I don't want other films, I don't want new films, I want my *Mother India*... Tell me, has India really changed? Does nobody watch *Mother India* anymore?'

It was an extraordinary question coming from somebody who had never visited India and, therefore, did not know what India had 'changed' from; his India was frozen on a movie screen fraying at the edges of time.

I muttered something suitably inane about social evolution and new consumer tastes, but the man wasn't listening to my dissertation. Meanwhile, the blocks flew past, 1500 K Street, 1600... I was a minute away.

He was far away, staring blankly at the road ahead, contemplating a nostalgic idyll that perhaps never was, lost in the memory of *Mother India* or perhaps Father Ethiopia; maybe both. Before I knew it, he had burst into tears. Seconds from my destination, full of questions on the Indo-US nuclear deal and the Congressional process that would make or break it, with a dozen chores to run before I took that train to Penn Station, I was stuck with a weeping taxi driver.

'Umm... er... Are you okay? Is all well? Can I help?'

'You're going home to India, you said; they still watch *Mother India* in India, you said...'

'Well, yes. Some people do.'

'I'll write down my address, can you mail me the DVD or CD... Deduct the money from the fare, don't pay me what it'll cost you.'

Without waiting for a response, almost before he'd pulled up, he tore off a slip of paper and wrote out his name and address. From indifference and semi-inquisitiveness, I now found myself feeling small and silly, taken aback that this man had been so touched, his life so altered, by a film from a country and a culture and a sensibility that I thought was mine alone. I insisted on paying him full fare, stuffed his address into my pocket and promised him his *Mother India*.

Moments later, I walked past the door at No. 1800, and rode up to the offices of a leading Washington think-tank, ready with queries on India's economic leverage, its strategic footprint, foreign policy influence, place in the world.

Somewhere on K Street, was an Ethiopian-American movie buff driving away with my answers?

Musings on a Mobike

PALDEN GYALSTEN

The barber is taking liberties with the straggly growth on my chin. He nonchalantly lops a few strands from above my ears too. I remember telling the fellow about beard trimming. Maybe my beard extends to beyond my ears. Or maybe he is dissatisfied with the growth on my face. Whatever. I'm mesmerized with the fellow's antics. He bellows something to somebody across the road. It's a fine morning, 7.30 a.m., in a side-lane in Delhi and I'm sitting on a rickety-chair under the sky and gazing at myself in a mirror hung on some V.I.P.'s backyard wall.

Say hello to me. A retired bureaucrat. No. More factually, a voluntarily retired bureaucrat. Age 43. Male. Sex occasionally. I was not pushed out of a trapdoor into the abyss at the age of sixty. I leapt into the void as a matter of choice. I have a streak of destructive energy in me. Maybe I'm a little masochistic too, but more on that later. The world loves a good drama and the latest trend is suicide bombers. Big loud bang and lots of gore everywhere. Voluntary retirement is a form of hara-kiri, only, in my case, there was no loud bang, no drama, except a little puddle on the street. The one I left as I wet my pants jumping into the void.

Three months down the line, I'm jobless; I still have some pennies in my pocket and am getting a bad beard job done on me. The occasional haircut is gratis. Thanks to the kind young vociferous barber. He is still on full volume to the chaiwallah across the street, obviously more interested in breaking his fast, having already broken my faith in his tradecraft. The cloth he's wrapped around my chest is dirty ochre. I avert my eyes after one shy glance at the loathsome thing. These roadside barbers are notoriously touchy. They hate any suggestion that they are less than hygienic. They can easily ask you to take a hike and there are no doors to be opened and shut with a bang as a sign of protest. I swallow my aversion and submit to god and his scissors.

I wanted to ease my way into this part of my life. I think I'll need a bit more grease and butter to do that. Transition is always rocky. Now I'm stocking up on the grease and butter.

My notice to the Government of India that I planned to seek voluntary retirement was signed on 15th August 2006. No prizes for guessing why, unless you are an American.

One evening I found myself feeding momos to Beni Ram, a patwari in Manali. We had met barely an hour before and no, we were not smashed on Manali dope. Yes, we had a couple of large vodkas. No, we are not gay. So, how can you explain a given set of actions on a particular day? Karma. Beni Ram owes me one now. One day in the IAS, the next day out on the road. Karma. The concept of Karma is one of the favorite whipping posts of the losers in the world. Let me add a few lashes to this comic cosmic drama.

It has been a meditative ride through the country. The rhythm of the road gets to you. Riding an Enfield has always been a one-of-a-kind pleasure for me. Having one between the legs for ten hours is a pain in the ass, literally. I now think I can give President Bush, a run for his money on the leathery ass competition.

It's funny in a way. A long road journey on a motorcycle is by itself a form of meditation. You have to be there in the moment. You cannot dream or regurtitate the past for too long or you are liable to be ambulanced. Your mind is spared unnecessary activity and gets the rest it so badly deserves. You also need to wear thin cotton pants and jockies otherwise a small crease can play havoc with your President Bush after a few hours.

I have totally fallen in love with the dirty, greasy beings we call mechanics. They are known as a breed of swindlers and charlatans. To my mind, no nobler creature exists in this world. In two different states of the country, three different mechanics did minor jobs on the motorcycle and each of them waved away the proferred money. They just liked the idea of the all-India drive that I'm on, or maybe I look too poor to pay. My opinion on this breed of princes will remain the same till I find a real bastard among them. The karmic network tells me that I will find the bugger soon.

It was a good run in the IAS till I found that I was not taking the job seriously and had started taking myself too seriously. That was taking the relationship between the job and myself on the negative foot and a bad human being will not make a good public servant. Time to call it quits. Thank you and goodbye. I'm still way too enamoured with myself but the mechanics and the barbers and the dhaba-owners will see me through.

Somewhere in a dhaba in West Bengal, I went to irrigate the fields behind it and slipped and fell on their garbage heap. Not many people can imagine a dhaba's garbage heap, but let me tell you, it looks and smells worse than a normal garbage pile. I had the pleasure of rubbing my President Bush on the squashy, squishy, multi-coloured mess.

The entire dhaba clan came to my rescue and I was hosed down on this extremely hot day. Thank God for the hot weather and the open motorcycle. The clothes were quickly dry except the area around President Bush. All this does wonders for chipping away at the stuffy old frog inside me.

'*Om Ah Hung Vajra Guru Padma Siddhi Hung*' is the root mantra of the Nyingmapa sect of Tibetan Buddhism. This sect is the prevalent one in Sikkim, where my home is. This is my constant prayer throughout the journey. There have been some nasty moments in the journey and I take refuge in the mantra. Even on good days and in every place I recite the mantra in the hope that there is wisdom and compassion in that place and in the world. In a few select places I perform the puja called the Rewo Sang Cho or the diamond practice. This needs a special preparation of three white and three sweet substances, medicines, incense etc. This prolongs life and removes obstacles, particularly those associated with unpaid karmic debts. The whole point of this journey is to try and pay back unpaid karmic debts. A puja to help speed up the process is a bonus.

One of my dreams has always been to learn Tai-Chi. I found a school in Chennai and did the basics over ten days. What fun this is. Freedom to do as I please, stay where I want to and learn the things that matter. I'm lousy at Tai-Chi. Hopefully, I will be able to devote more time to it in the future. But, hey, one step taken is one step taken. It's such a graceful art and pretty hard on the hips and legs. I would recommend it to all ages.

Tim Heinemann is a ding-dong entrepreneur. An ex-hippie. He showed me the beauty of a night sky in Tiripur, Tamil Nadu. There are lots of stars in the sky, if you care to look carefully. We slept on his roof-top after he had sniffed the speed and direction of the wind that night. Like a general, he organized our defences against the huge mosquitoes by burning red mosquito repellant tablets. These had to be placed at exactly the right height and direction to get maximum coverage over the thin mattresses on the ground. We slept after eating a dinner of twelve eggs and two loaves of brown bread. Talk about American excesses. Even if he is a naturalized Indian. Childhood habits, I guess. There were no fans working inside Tim's small rented house, so the roof-top was a natural setting on that hot April night. When Tim makes ding the cash register rings and when he makes dong, you sleep on his roof-top. He is into garments and has a lovely temperament and a large heart.

I've found that life favours me with twenty-year phases—give or take a few years. The first twenty years I was essentially a student and a son. The second phase, beginning from twenty-two, I was a father, husband and a bureaucrat. I've no idea where the third phase, beginning at forty three, is leading me to, but I look forward to it with some degree of animation as well as trepidation. I really have not been too successful in any role but will give myself an average score. Most of us rate that anyway. Life cannot be just this. Life needs to give one some answers. If the answers don't come, most people tend to forget the questions. A few go in search of the answers and among them most will die confused. At least they tried.

Osama Bin Laden is a big shining mirror in the sky. He is just a reflection of the internal terrorist in each one of us. The terrorist self decides on the political, social and economic code for us. He even decides what goes on in the mind. We are frightened and desperate and we stay under his protection. To kill your own Osama is a dicey task. Think about it. There are ways of non-violent annihilation of your own Osama. And you don't need the help of your own President Bush to do it.

I've looked death in the eyes two times already. One was for a longish period of two years when I had hepatitis C. Once was just for a few seconds as I rolled down the hill in a four-wheel drive. Death blinked first, both times. The son of a gun will get me someday. That's for sure. Having seen it first-hand at such close quarters, I got down with a vengeance to sort out my priorities. Chucking up the job and riding without aim is part of the psychological meltdown. I think I'm the proverbial cat. That means I have seven times more before old Dr Death gets me.

The whole system of financial rewards for the bureaucracy is palpably funny. After serving for more than twenty years in the IAS, I got twelve lakh as bye-bye money out of which I had to pay back eight lakh towards my house-building loan. Net worth Rs four lakh. Crazy. I still have some of the loose change in my pocket right now after three months on the road. This alone was reason to jump ship on time. I think the eunuchs that I met in Dindigul made more money.

The eunuch and gay community of Dindigul took me warmly into their community for the four hours I spent with them. Too warmly, in fact, for my comfort. They have a subterranean life as well, other than what we see. Some of them claim to be married to men, but live separately for society's sake. Some live with a married couple—more like threesomes. Some are sex workers and some just like the joyous life of a eunuch. The eunuchs are the top of the hierarchy, followed by *satla kothie* i.e. transvestites (cross-dressers) and then come the double-deckers (both ways with men) and the bi-sexual and finally the *kothi* (passive) and the *panthies* (active). Seems to me their social structure is built on the bureaucratic one. Some give, some take, some give and take, and most are cross-dressers anyway.

The first phase of the journey was rudely interrupted by the Hon. Supreme Court which had issued summons to me to appear before it on April 27th 2007 on a contempt case. Four other secretaries to the government of Kerala also stood along with me in those familiar surroundings. Since there was some progress in the case, the Hon. Supreme Court has dispensed with my presence for the time being. The claws of the bureaucracy continue to bite into my ribs even after my retirement. God only knows how long before I'm finally and fully left off the hook for serving the people of this nation. Take a hint and serve yourself.

Fouta Unbound

KRITI SHARMA

Wedged in the back seat of a *taxi brousse* that was bouncing along a dusty potholed mud track at 60 km an hour, I wondered if I would ever reach Ourossogui. Basking like a lazy lizard in the strong, scorching African sun, Ourossogui is a small town tucked away in the remote arid north-eastern Fouta region of Senegal. Strategically situated 7 km from the Mauritanian border, this small town is a crucial trade junction and an odd place for a nineteen-year-old Indian girl to visit.

I had reached Senegal's coastal capital a few weeks earlier as the monsoon played hide-and-seek with Dakar. Armed with the intention of doing something more than just frittering away my summer holidays, I had volunteered to work with a non-governmental organization (NGO) in Senegal and discover Senghor's country. As a young student embarking on my first journey on African soil, I was ready for adventure but nothing could have prepared me for the Fouta region.

The traditionally conservative Fouta region is witness to practices such as child marriage and female genital cutting (FGC), which are fairly widespread and common. Pulaar culture prescribes FGC/excision as an obligatory pre-nuptial rite. Every young girl is subjected to this procedure before marriage, sometimes at the early age of six. Contrary to Western misconceptions, this practice is not inflicted on daughters by cruel uncaring mothers, but is carried out in blind deference to custom with a desire to protect a daughter's honour, avoid social stigma and get her a suitable match. Although Islam does not advocate FGC, in the local mindset it is often associated with religion. This makes it harder to eradicate. My NGO had been working for the empowerment of these communities through informal education, with a programme geared to making communities voluntarily abandon the practice. It was my task to evaluate the success of this venture in a few villages of the Fouta region. Fascinated by the Pulaar people and their culture, I could not wait to discover the area.

Even before the first rays of sunlight had nudged Dakar awake, I had made my way sleepy-eyed to the *gare routière*, a huge terminus for all kinds of vehicles. Picking my way over slushy ground dotted with old rusted vehicles and garbage, I found the Ourossogui *taxi brousse*. The most common mode of intercity transport in Senegal is the renting of a seat on a station wagon known as a *taxi brousse*. These cars have two rows of seats and can accommodate seven passengers plus the driver. Dragging my bag behind me, I looked around for the person in charge of the taxi. A bearded man with a large belly bustled towards me; his sheer size was enough to tell me that he would be a tough one to bargain with. I was prepared to pay the fixed price of 10,000 CFA (approximately $20) for my seat to Ourossogui but it was on the price paid for the baggage that the money was made. Taking in my foreign appearance at one glance, he quoted the exorbitant price of 1500 CFA for one piece of luggage. Not one to be taken for a ride, I stood my ground and bargained like a true Indian until he agreed to the price of 500 CFA. My ethnic salwar kameez was similar to the tunics worn by Senegalese women and the fact that I spoke fluent French worked in my favour. On a shoestring budget as a volunteer, the money saved was important, of course, but I had discovered that over and above the pecuniary aspect, bargaining was more like a greeting, and expected behaviour. To refuse to play the game would have been downright rude.

Settling down in the back seat of the rickety *taxi brousse* I curiously eyed my fellow passengers. A grumpy middle-aged math teacher occupied the front seat. It was an unspoken rule in Senegal that the most comfortable seat next to the driver was chauvinistically reserved for men. A sickly old lady, a nun from Chad and a Senegalese woman with a baby on holiday from France filled the second row. The car would not leave until it was full; I whiled away my time until two more passengers bought the seats next to me in the back row built for two people. As it turned out, a businessman in a jet-black suit and a large African mama from Mauritania were destined to be squashed in next to me. After an hour and a half of heavy negotiation with the driver while the rest of us waited patiently, the Mauritanian woman climbed in next to me, well satisfied that all her large sacks of colourful stuffed toys were loaded onto the roof of the car. Her ample proportions overflowing onto me, she thrust various packets and an old radio on my lap for me to hold for her for the next thirteen hours. I meekly complied.

Instead of using the highway, we bounced along narrow winding village roads. Our driver was strange, to say the least. Chewing on kola nuts, he refused to explain the route he took despite protests and angry queries from the gang sitting behind him. From time to time, he would veer off the road into a field where, seemingly out of nowhere, a man would appear, run alongside the vehicle and either take a parcel from our driver or hand him one!

Throughout the journey food preoccupied the passengers. At every gas station women laden with goodies would rush towards the taxi, pushing and shoving each other. Not surprisingly, the product most in demand was water. Small plastic bags of frozen water were handed out to thirsty passengers; tearing off one corner of the bag, passengers sucked on the bag like an ice-lolly. Everything, from juicy ripe mangoes to sugar-coated peanuts to fritters was bargained for. In true African style, the food was generously shared while an intense political discussion about the forthcoming elections added spice to the meal.

I dozed off to the rhythm of Senegalese music wafting over the radio and to the sound of the voice of the nun from Chad who was recounting her adventures. As I fanned myself to sleep, I felt strangely at home.

On arrival, I instantly made friends with Abou Diack, the lanky six-foot-five man in his mid-forties who came to pick me up on behalf of my organization. Deported at the age of fourteen from Mauritania by the Moors' racist regime, Abou Diack was living proof that ethnic issues rather than ideology governed large parts of Africa even today.

Covered in dust and with windswept tangled hair after my thirteen-hour journey, I accompanied Abou Diack to the office to meet everyone. My home in Ourossogui consisted of a small dusty yellow room in the office compound. Caddo, the caretaker, and his wife Fama, lived in the room next to mine. The office being partly closed for the summer, the only other person there was Kadidia, a tall, pretty soft-spoken lady with whom I would soon share a girlie camaraderie.

My family in Ourossogui also included the animal kingdom. I shared my bathing water with insects, my room with cockroaches and my bed with mosquitoes. Instead of being disgusted at this invasion of my space, I rather liked it this way because it gave me the feel that I was roughing it out. A mission in rural Africa was supposed to be tough and reaching Africa had been a quest for me. I felt like the deep purple and orange chameleons that strutted about the office compound, proud to have made it up to here and willing to adapt to any situation.

Bouncing along behind Abou Diack on a motorcycle, I went on my first field trip to Matam, the route winding its way through a protected forest. An hour later, Abou Diack and I were sitting on the floor of a local women's leader's house in a circle with eight other women who had benefited from my NGO's programme. On a continent that had been exploited for centuries by Western imperialist forces, the people had found a way of taking development into their own hands instead of waiting for the government to take action. Women were fast becoming the engines of community activity and the agents of social change. Not only had they taken a strong stance against FGC, they had also managed to get the support of their local imam. Edging their way into the male-dominated society, they were now not only socio-economic but also political actors. The women leaders I met were energetic and determined to keep their development in their own hands.

My next stop was Sédo Sébé, a Wolof village in the Pulaar-dominated Fouta region. Traditionally, the Wolof do not practice female genital cutting, but since Sédo Sébé is in the heart of a Pulaar region, they are obliged to follow the Pulaar custom in order to intermarry. The nearby village of Ser Abas, along with other surrounding villages, had recently made a public declaration in which they had announced their abandonment of the practice of FGC. Since other villages had also stopped the practice, intermarriage was still possible. After such a public statement there was no going back. This certainly had a stimulating effect on Sédo Sébé.

Sédo Sébé is a prosperous village of farmers. The younger generation is often educated abroad, in France or Italy, but the elders tend to cling to tradition. That afternoon we had lunch with a group of people who followed my NGO's programme. I was surprised to find that the men in the group were very liberal-minded and sometimes even keener on women's liberation, as it is phrased in the West, than the women themselves. Abou Diack, too, was a strong supporter of the emergence of feminine leadership in the region. The stereotype of the oppressed African woman was definitely not true in this part of Senegal.

Abou Diack did not seem to enjoy the Wolof food that we were served in Sédo Sébé very much. I, on the other hand, had been homesick for Wolof food ever since I reached the Fouta. At the Dakar office we had eaten Senegalese style, all seated on the floor on a mat around a large platter that we shared. The food usually consisted of a platter piled high with steaming rice on the top of which perched a whole fish surrounded by fried onions, carrots, cabbage, potato and yam. This popular national dish is known as *ceebu jen*, which is the name for a dish of rice cooked with fish. The rice had a unique crunchy texture and the fish and vegetables contributed to the taste. Meat was more expensive and although it was popular in upper middle-class homes, elsewhere it was more of a delicacy or a part of festive meals. In the Ourossogui office, I had a harder time adapting to the food. Couscous was much more popular in the Fouta and they did not cook the food in the thick finger-licking gravies that I relished.

Moreover, in the evenings we ate dinner in the courtyard under the stars. All very picturesque and exotic except for the sand blown by the wind into the food. I gorged on the food in Sédo Sébé, my oasis in the middle of the sweltering Sahel.

My daily rides with Abou Diack to different villages had now become a routine. In the beginning, I had had trouble adjusting to riding on the back of a motorbike on bumpy roads for over 20 km at a stretch and my back would ache. However, Abou Diack found me a snazzy helmet with sun protection and soon, my hair streaming flag-like in the wind, I thoroughly enjoyed the rides, even when they were longer. I loved the scenery and feasted my eyes on the herds of wild stallions that would gallop across the road. The sides of the road were also often littered with carcasses of dogs, sheep, oxen or horses. Abou Diack blamed the late monsoon for this. It was proof that everything in the Sahel was at the mercy of the weather. Indeed, Ourossogui was much hotter than anything I had ever been used to; temperatures bordered on 50°C and a breeze was rare. My room had only a table fan. However, with only one plug point in my room, I was faced with a constant dilemma: charge my cell phone to keep in touch with my family, or use the precious plug point for the table fan, my only source of relief from the heat. It was of course the fan that won hands down.

The only positive aspect of the weather was that my clothes dried within half an hour of washing them. In Dakar, my Senegalese co-workers and I had shared a flat and they had watched with an eagle eye for the least sign of clumsiness in my technique. My Senegalese colleagues would get frustrated watching the inexperienced American volunteers struggle with their laundry and would offer to do it for them. I, on the other hand, passed the test and was allowed to do my own laundry. In Ourossogui, Fama would stand over me and watch while I washed my clothes. I found it unnerving but I knew this was important to get into her good books. I enjoyed these moments because Fama and I got to know each other through this. It would be an overstatement to say that we communicated but we did speak to each other, only in different languages. I would ask her how to get rid of the slushy mud stains on my clothes splashed by the back tyre of the bike. I assume she responded by recommending a solution but since I spoke in French and she in Pulaar, I would just keep nodding, pretending to take her advice. Since Fama was the only person in the Ourossogui office who did not speak French it took us longer to become friends. The night she invited me to dance with her husband and herself, I knew I had passed the litmus test.

Under a clear starry sky the three of us danced to the rhythm of traditional Pulaar beats that their battered squeaky radio produced while the moonlight made patterns on the courtyard floor. Caddo translated Fama's very seriously given advice to me: if I wanted to catch a good husband I must learn to dance with my hips, African style. The first question I had been asked upon exiting the Dakar airport and ever since, was if I was married. I would answer without batting an eyelid that I had been happily married for two years whether this question came from neighbours or shopkeepers. The reason for this well-practised lie was only because it sometimes became very difficult to reject marriage proposals from complete strangers without offending them. Strange as it may sound, in Senegal, young girls, especially foreign ones, are propositioned seriously for marriage by totally unknown men.

My work was going smoothly. When I was not visiting villages I taught my office colleagues how to use different programmes such as Excel, Acrobat, Adobe on the computer. It was a new experience for me as well because I had to start from the very basics explaining what the right and left keys on the mouse were for. By the end of it, my 'students' were scanning pictures of themselves, using Skype to communicate with the Dakar office and even printing out diplomas for the completion of their computer course!

The highlight of my trip was undoubtedly my meeting the visionary village chief of Katoté, a lush green village not far from Sédo Sébé. I had dressed carefully for the occasion, choosing a long skirt that reached my ankles. My organization had advised me to avoid wearing trousers and to dress in skirts and traditional Senegalese clothes so as to fit in with the conservative culture of the Fouta. Abou Diack and I sat with the chief under a thatched pergola in the courtyard of the best hut in the village while I interviewed the chief. His large family of two wives and eight children was asked to sit under the other pergola while he spoke to us. His house was located at the entrance of the village; the house itself consisted of several huts and there was even a little hut that had been converted into a phone booth and had been placed at the disposal of the entire village. I soon learned that the chief had been educated in France and spoke French quite eloquently. He was everything I had imagined a village chief to be. He sat with great dignity on his divan, and just the way he held himself upright in his majestic blue robes, distinguished him from the other people in the village. He wore a *boubou*, the traditional Senegalese dress that resembles a loose caftan.

My days in the Fouta were fast coming to an end and I had

become so attached to the region and my little family there that I could not imagine leaving. My co-workers were also reluctant to let me go. Volunteers rarely came to Ourossogui as it was remote and generally too hot for American interns to handle. Little did I know that the universe had contrived to make my journey back easier. By the time Abou Diack dropped me off at the road terminus, it had rained, making the ride back much cooler. And as I was to discover, I was not going to be travelling alone as I had a self-appointed escort in the form of a mouse who accompanied me to Dakar by hiding in the lining of my handbag! By the time I reached bustling Dakar I was extremely nostalgic but I knew that Ourossogui was so deeply engraved in my heart that I would definitely go back there.

Can't Please Anyone

SHUBHRA GUPTA

I come out, blinking, into bright sunlight. Just finished watching a film. It's a Friday. Movie day. Go tearing off towards the car. Have to head to town, to a theatre far, far away, for the second film.

Bump into, ulp, the gentleman I have replaced at my paper as the film critic. Said person, having been supplanted after many years of holding sway over his column inches, greets me warmly. We've known each other a while and we enjoy what they call cordial relations, but no one likes being told they are not wanted any more. Still, we smile at each other when we meet, as we often do.

He says, with a convivial arm around my shoulder, '*Toh kaisi lagi* (How was the movie)?' I mumble, like I always do, something noncommittal. Hate being pounced on for snap judgements—how many creative ways *are* there to say crap? It's only been a while, and I'm having to be super-inventive already.

He grins, moves away a little, and says: 'Tell me, do, or I'll have to read you, and you know I can't understand all the intellectual stuff you write.'

There. He's said it. It's been around, his comment, bobbing along on subterranean currents amongst fellow critics and colleagues. I look at him. He gazes back, a much older, grizzled veteran of film festivals and debates and open forums. I refuse to pick up the gauntlet, slip-slide away.

*

That happened more than seventeen years ago, when I was just stepping into the life of a professional movie reviewer/critic/writer. Those days it was easy to find an editor who would look around a newsroom, ask if anyone was free, and send them off to the latest release. Pretty much like how flower shows and dog shows were routinely handed over to the newest cub reporter who just happened to be female—movies didn't require a gender preference, just an air of general uselessness.

I had logged in some years in a couple of newsrooms by then, done my share of reporting on crime and courts and colleges, and what people these days call breaking news. Back then, it would go somewhat like this.

It is the end of a long day, around 1 a.m., and the night reporter calls in an accident. How many dead? We halt in our tracks, cars idling in the porch of the building from which issued Delhi's largest-selling newspaper, all set to go home. We are in the dead zone, sleep-deprived zombies who will reach home at some point, to keep our date with dawn. No one thinks it is an insensitive question. Only two? Not worth taking now. Put it on the desk, on top of the hold-over: those were the days when there were no computers, and when we left work, our clothes stank of the molten lead used in the presses.

Only life at the movies can be as surreal. Or as bizarre. I left the grind of daily journalism behind gladly, just about the time bulky computers began replacing our trusty rusty Remingtons, and became a weekly person. On Friday, when the weekend loomed ahead, when everyone in sane nine-to-five jobs was winding down, I'd be all cranked up. Watching films all day, sometimes late into the night, back to back, rushing in and out of musty movie halls—no multiplexes those days—eyes streaming.

Bliss.

*

Long back, an old film critic wrote somewhere: we are all critics of film, only, some of us write about it. Those words, like the acerbic comment from my long-time fellow critic, have stayed. Being dubbed an unreadable intellectual is only part of it—when you are out there, living by your opinion, know this—you are fair game for those who do not agree with you.

And we are all argumentative Indians. We love movies. We love getting in there, first day, first show, licking our chops, getting our feet wet, going berserk. We love discussing the film threadbare. And we love lighting into those who dare to tell us what we should watch. Or not.

So here I am, having notched up a few years in the business. And there's this movie which has newly arrived in theatres after a year's slow burn. It's like, you know, a Barjatya film. Which means it is bound to star good girls, good boys, and cruel fate. But it is also the follow-up film of Sooraj B, the young reclusive director who redefined the definition of youthful romance with his debut, in which carrier pigeons played as important a role as the hero and heroine.

We troop into *Hum Aapke Hain Koun...!* Madhuri, in her passion-purple blouse, dances on to the screen, and seduces us in an instant. Amazingly vital, alive, her smile a sunburst. She dances on. Everyone bursts into song every couple of minutes. The purple changes to green. She keeps dancing. Salman is as coquettish as his lady love—in those days he didn't mumble as much, so we could actually hear what he said. There are no pigeons, but there is a poodle being kept very busy.

I think, hang on, what do I think? That Madhuri is stunning? Check. That you can't have a series of songs strung together in syrup and call it a movie? Check. We've got our *sagaai, sangeet, mehndi, shaadi* videos (this was much before VCDs and DVDs) stashed away at the back of our wardrobes, where they will moulder away just like those unused wedding gifts—all those hideous silver tumblers, and brass table lamps. Who watches wedding videos once it's all said and done? Who will watch this movie?

So, so wrong. About 200 million people proved that I didn't know what I was talking about. Keep your Fassbinders and de Sicas and Fellinis, and Rays and Ghataks and Sens, and also your Benegals in your glass cases. This, now *this* was a movie. About *Bharatiya sanskriti* and culture (this was much, much before MTV arrived). This is How We Were and Who We Wanted To Be, All Over Again. It went on to make multiples of crores, an impossible sum in those days when balcony tickets in metro theatres cost eighteen rupees. Some of the tonier establishments, which had emerged relatively unscathed from the bloodbath of the 1980s ('*Filmon mein aajkal kya rakha hai ji, sirf* sex *aur* violence, *isse accha toh ghar baith ke* video *dekho*': I heard this everywhere I went those days) charged a princely twenty-five rupees.

Word on the street was that young Sooraj, grandson of the

fabled Tarachand, made sure that the theatres which wanted to run his movie, had chairs which weren't falling apart, and rats which only scurried underneath, not leapt into your lap, and clean loos. It was, after all, nearly four hours long. It started slow, hunkered down, and didn't leave. At New Delhi's Delite, it ran fifty-two straight weeks, picking up new viewers and providing succour to devotees on the way. Crazed fans returned over and over again, to watch Madhuri thrust her pert posterior in their faces.

So what do I know from anything? You got box office, who needs crrrrrritics?

'*Arrey,* she hardly likes a thing.' This, from an old-time PRO, Omprakash Katiyal, a spare, smiley gent who appeared to have been around since movies began. (This is way before all the smart young things from natty corp comm. agencies came into existence, whose standard line, just when one is about to rush into a screening, slays me everytime: 'Are you from the press?'). In all the years I have been infesting theatres, he's never once given up a chance to tell me gently: 'Write something nice. Oh, all right, if you can't say anything nice, at least don't say anything bad.' He knows it's never going to happen, but that's not going to stop him from doing his job.

He's a lovely man, Om P. He still calls Saturday mornings, listens to what I have to say (in the early days I would make the mistake of telling him exactly what I thought, and have my head chewed off) and then tries to get me to change my mind, by telling me what others critics have told him. They are, of course, all praise for the movie, so why do I alone have to be difficult? He can, when he is in the mood, recite whole swatches from *Mughal-e-Azam,* and has sung Dilip Kumar's songs on the phone to me: what he lacks in tunefulness, he makes up with his sheer verve.

There have been times when he has been less affable. 'I don't know what all she writes,' he has muttered, not quite out of earshot, inclusive of some colourful expletives in Hindi which he spreads around with ease, especially with old cohorts like me. 'The other one gave it four stars,' he's added, holding up the corresponding number of fingers, referring to a fellow critic's column. He's not the only one who dislikes the fact that my reviews go without ratings, which just means that you have to read the darn thing to rate the film yourself. Come on, now, confess, once you've seen a single 'star' above a review, do you really bother to read further?

Stars, stripes, bouquets and bricks—measuring out the years from one Friday to another, does strange things to your head. When people ask, as they tend to, so what did you see last week, I blank out. Last week? When was that? I don't remember.

Because I've trained my brain to forget. Once I'm done watching and writing, the movie is gone. Recessed into the hard disc in my computer. Only sometimes it stays in my head, to sit around till I want it fetched again.

Back when I began, no one watched Hindi movies. Or at least did not confess to the fact. The choice to 'do' Bollywood, as opposed to say, Hollywood (we still don't get too much from other countries as commercial releases) was, in a way, no choice. Hindi movies speak to me because they are mine. Bollywood turned cool when we moved out of the 1990s. Since then I've been deemed cool too. I'm asked if I want company to press shows, a lot. It's another matter that my companions, mostly in their exuberant twenties, spend more time concentrating on their cellphones than on celluloid. For most of them, it's more about being able to say, 'Hey I've seen that one already!'

And I get upbraided a lot too. A text conversation I had last year with a journalist friend who has been in the profession as long as I have, is saved in my phone. 'When you say no one laughed,' he messaged, at the crack of dawn on a Sunday morning, 'those people must have been critics'. It seems he had laughed his head off himself, watching it, and so had his wife and kids. It was some supposed comedy, which I'd thought was dreary and laboured and trite and remarkably unfunny.

'You critics,' he sneered in his next message, 'always missing the popular mood, always looking for intelligent movies'.

I picked up the phone, and got into a heated exchange. With him, I could. He's an old friend, a long-time print man, having recently got into TV and begun thinking in terms of sound bytes (I've lost count of the number of eager TV reporters who fetch up for bytes, with me politely refusing, having no desire to be appear instantly all-knowing). He refused to see my point of view; I his. The standoff continues, cheerfully.

And it's not always that I get slammed/ knocked for saying the movie was plain ghastly. There have been times that I've liked a movie, and I've had to field reactions like, 'How could you? It was terrible!' It happened again, just recently, with ad-man turned first time filmmaker R. Balki's *Cheeni Kum*, which presents Amitabh as irascible chef cum grey-haired, pony-tailed boyfriend of Tabu. I liked the idea of having a grown man, not a callow boy, as a full-fledged, ticket-carrying lover; I liked some of the lines, and some of the execution. Net net, its good outweighed the bad. Not for this friend, also a faithful reader of mine. 'I cursed you,' she said. And laughed. That made it a little better. But only just.

Those hundreds of movies I have seen, for the most part, have been shared experiences with paying movie-goers. The first-day-first-show crowd, the ones who stand in line, elbows gripping the ticket counter firmly so that no other hand can slip in, rushing into the hall as soon as the doors open, led in by ushers who have been around for years, who know I like centre-side seats.

You are part of them, that amorphous audience that the filmmaker woos every day of his working life. Will they come? Will they keep coming? Or will they, through some sort of osmosis, sniff out that this one is a shocker, and stay away? One of the enduring mysteries of the trade is how a clunker, even in the first show, is deserted: the audience always knows.

*

In all these years of taking it on the chin—you need to know how to do that, if you dish it out, week after week—I remember only one instance of naked aggression. I was at a Diwali *mela*, doing the rounds with family, when this bunch of people I'd recently met loomed ahead. One of them, a director whose first film had been roundly rejected the past Friday, spat at me furiously: how dared I write such a nasty review? If it hadn't been for the others, I have no doubt he would have struck me.

It left me shaken. And thinking. To make a film is quite an enterprise: to get together the money, the talent, the locations, the sets, the props, the technicians, and a story—that last one is usually on the casualty list of those who come bopping into Movie City, intent on making *that* movie—all of this and more have to be put into place, much before the finished article can come onscreen.

A negative word, even if it is well balanced, appears like a death sentence. Even the bigger production houses, which have the wherewithal to release a thousand prints at one fell swoop to mop up that crucial first weekend profit, get hot under their increasingly corporate collars these days when they see anything that's less than a gush affair.

But, and this is the thing, I'm not in this to give anyone a hand job. I'm in this because I love movies. I love getting out on Fridays, and walking into the first movie of the day, having heard the worst things about it, or knowing that it is going to be one of those during which I will have to invest my soul with vast amounts of patience. I go into the second, and the third, and the fourth, and very often, the fifth, all in one day. I finish sometimes late into the night. Exhausted, but exhilarated. The duds get the same amount of attention as the ones that soar and sing. Because I know how hard it is to make a movie, I take my job very, very seriously.

It is, after all, my job. I am as objective as a passionate person can be, but I am always rooting for the movies, and the people who make them.

*

I've lost count of the number of girls who've swooned, 'Oh, I luuuurve Shah Rukh, can I come with you when you meet him next?' Now it's John, but you get the point. There will always be someone I meet at parties who will say, 'Oh you must be talking to all the stars all the time, no?' Well, actually, no. I don't meet stars. I don't get invited to their parties. They are not on the phone to me, confiding their deepest secrets, willing me to spill them on print. All these glamorous things happen to people who 'cover' stars as celebrities. They are the ones who get called to their palatial homes for celebratory kebabs and biryanis, or get asked if they want to accompany them on exotic foreign shoots: better to do the interview over a setting sun, on a beach, accompanied by a pink drink with a tiny umbrella floating on top, no?

This is what *I* do. I watch their films when they release. And I write what I think of the films, and their performances: not about them, and their latest amours, or their endorsements.

Sometimes, though, when I see my questioner's face fall, I tell them about my (very brief) encounters with stars. They leave, reassured, basking in the reflected glory of the body who has shared space with real, live superstars.

I *have* met a few, on and off. And my takeaway has been pretty much the same as those others who meet stars specifically around the time their new films are on release, when they are on promotional tours, forced into being nice to a gaggle of strangers. Some have nothing much to say: Madhuri has a more infectious giggle than Sridevi, and much the more dazzling smile, but conversations with them—hmm, well, you have to do all the hard work. (These encounters were way back in the very early 1990s when they were both top stars, and cut-throat rivals who smiled prettily at the mention of the other.) I remember Preity Zinta, very far from being the star she turned out to be, on her Delhi visit around Mani Ratnam's *Dil Se*, sitting cross-legged on the bed in her hotel room, tucking into a huge platter of something which consisted of bread and veggies. She was hungry, could she eat, and *then* do the Q and A?

These are people who live in fish bowls, under constant

scrutiny, and always have to be ready with an answer which will satisfy the questioner. And sometimes, you can empathize when they just flick back their hair (all female film stars have to flick back their hair, or smooth it back, with *both* hands, at the same time: it's a law), and smile, and say nothing: how much can you say when you are confronted with that dreaded 'How did you like working with So-and-So?'

Meanwhile, I wince, fold my notebook—and later, when I acquired it, switch off my Sony Dictaphone—and swear I will never waltz into these circuses again.

But some things are worth the effort, even when you're waiting around for the presser to begin, or the film star to descend from her room, after decompressing from that delayed flight, and lost luggage, and sometimes, famously, a hangover. Shah Rukh's razor-sharp wit, Aamir's measured responses, Salman's funny retorts: okay, there are your three Khans. The very cultured Abhishek who stands up when you enter the room, Anil Kapoor, who turns out pretty *au courant* with the day's happenings, and what has appeared in your newspaper. 'You do know that your editor is a good friend of mine, right?' he tells you. Actually, I do. He makes time for me, we chat, he goes off for the next shot. I come home.

But I do have a couple of stories I still dine on. The first stars Govinda. And the second has Amitabh, with Govinda in the background. This was, again, back in the 1990s. It happened in one of those farmhouses south of South Delhi which had a stream running through the grounds, and a moat surrounding it, and gargoyles which dotted the excessively tall hedges. We were waiting for the man, some of us old print hands, but the real numbers were made up by the newly-ascendant television reporters and lacquered young ladies trailing microphones and wires.

78

It was nearly 11 pm. My favourite PRO looked at me looking at my watch, and said hurriedly, '*Govindaji bas aa hi rahein hain, ek aur* drink *ley lo, ji*'. It is an unwritten rule that in Bollywood parties, at least in Delhi, you are served whiskey or coke, there's nothing in between. I said no to more dark fizz, and settled back. Was about to doze off, when there was a stir. Govindaji, resplendent in black, strode past. He was smaller than he looked on screen, and surprisingly slimmer.

Half an hour later, the TV gang was still on. Gathering up a few of us neglected print types, I barged into the room. Some over-animated cutie was going on and on. I stepped in front of the camera. Govindaji, all pearly whites (he has the most perfect teeth, like all stars, except for Ajay Devgan, who, the one time I meet him, displayed a set that was stained indelibly brown) turned his back on the still-squawking creature. '*Nahin, nahin,* please *aap boliye,*' he told me. He was affable, he cracked jokes, he made sure we were mollified. As we left, another made-up girl trailing a microphone was adjusting her make-up. So was Govindaji.

This is my other one, and then I'm done.

This time it was *Bade Miyan* Amitabh with *Chote Miyan* Govinda, in David Dhawan's new film of the same name, which was supposed to resurrect the former's sagging career. But the sit rep was, regrettably, the same. A solid phalanx of TV reporters and related paraphernalia swamped the room. It was a Big Bollywood Party, and by now TV reporters were the real stars ('Madam, please wait a little, they're talking to the channelwallahs'). The film stars knew that. So there was Amitabh keeping pace with the nimbler Govinda, and there was no stopping the flashes, and the chatter.

There were five of us, all from 'esteemed' publications. But the TV juggernaut rolled on, till I raised my voice over the din, and said, 'Mr Bachchan, could you turn around, please.' Mr Bachchan broke off, wheeled towards us smoothly—he had to do a complete 360 degrees—and said, 'Let's talk to these people too.' The *Purabiya* touch raised a laugh, as he knew it would. Govinda, not wanting to be outdone by Bade Miyan, not even here, joined him quickly. And we got our ten minutes.

But I've saved the best part till the last. There's a post-conference dinner, and only some of us 'senior' film critics are invited to share Amitabh's table. There is a graceless scramble, and all the seats are filled. But I am not to be deterred, not tonight. So I perch on the arm of the chair closest to Amitabh: he is at the head of the table, naturally. I sit like that, for close to an hour and half, about ten inches away from his face, never once getting him to look at me straight. His eyes will cross if he tries. I don't quite remember what I ask, but he does answer a question, looking down at his plate. And I have my Amitabh moment.

*

Stars come. Stars go. But movies go on forever.

Khullam Khulla

AMAN SETHI

Sometimes, on a good day, when the photocopies are clear and unsullied, it is possible to imagine the contours, spaces and populace of a city by simply reading its city laws. Definitions, regulations, special provisions and possible offences build multiple worst-case scenarios of crime, chaos, indecent behaviour and wilful trespass, giving us insights into the waywardness of citizens, and the anxieties of administration. Municipal Acts, in this regard, are particularly revealing. By steering clear of the heinous, the treasonous and the sensational, municipal laws plot subtle sketches of the realm of ordinary, everyday law-breaking that we all inhabit.

Like any large city in India, Delhi too has her own legacy of laws, ordinances and court directives that, like cunning landmines, lie quietly in wait for a careless passerby. The incomplete list of Acts that govern the street in Delhi include the Madras Restriction of Habitual Offenders Act,1948, The Punjab Security of State Act, 1953, The Madras Dramatic Performances Act, 1954, The Delhi Public Gambling Act 1955, The Bombay Prevention of Begging Act, 1959 and the Delhi Police Act, 1978. These are acts that regulate 'the leading, driving, conducting or conveying [of] any elephant or wild or dangerous animal through or in any street', prescribe penalties for 'bathing or washing in places not set apart for the purpose', flying kites 'or any other thing so as [to] cause danger, injury or alarm to persons, animals or property', and 'being found under suspicious circumstances between sunrise and sunset'.[1]

A perusal of the various Delhi Acts formulated over the years leads the reader to two basic conclusions: one, that Delhi is an unruly and dangerous city where beggars, pickpockets and an indecent public lurch from 'places of amusement' to 'places of entertainment', uncouth youth deliver 'harangues, gestures and mimetic representations... [that] offend against decency and morality and undermine the security of the State'[2] and wild elephants roam the streets. And two, that the Municipal Corporation of Delhi (MCD) and the Delhi Police work overtime to contain the dark forces of chaos that threaten to engulf the city.

Bara Tooti labour chowk, Sadar Bazaar, exists right in the heart of this complex matrix of law and enforcement. It comprises a space where daily-wage labourers sit every morning in wait of employment that is provided by small-time contractors, home owners and shopkeepers. At any given time, the chowk hosts between twenty and two hundred labourers. While some workers live in nearby rented accommodation, most eat, sleep, work and live on the pavements—an act that in itself is illegal as it attracts penalties under Section 84 of the Delhi Police Act that, among others, prohibits the obstruction of pavements and footpaths. Apart from Section 84, the chowk is, in the eyes of the law, illegal and illegitimate under a host of other sections, subsections and clauses and yet it exists, survives and occasionally thrives. In this instance, the mandi is like so many different

---

[1] See Delhi Police Act, 1978.

[2] Quote taken from Chapter IV, Section 30 (f), Delhi Police Act, 1978

processes and agents that exist in Delhi in spite of the best efforts of upper middle-class groups like Resident Welfare Associations who file Public Interest Litigations, the Supreme Courts and the media. Editorials in newspapers such as the right-leaning *Indian Express*, bemoan how the authorities regularly turn a blind eye to all manners of violations, complain ceaselessly about how India is the most legislated, yet least enforced country in the world, and finally ask the big, poignant question: 'What are the police doing?'

Enter the Constable. 'Constable', according to the 'Definitions' section of the Delhi Police Act 1978, is 'a police officer of the lowest grade'—a job description that is as insulting as it is accurate. However, the local constable is perhaps the most essential cog in the law enforcement machinery. Close to the ground and 'the people', the constable often finds himself in the line of fire when the police are called upon 'to do something'. He is the most subordinate of the subordinate ranks, but, in terms of proximity, is the nearest organ of the surveillance and security apparatus of the state.

The constable is charged with dispelling discord, disorder and disruptions on his beat and imposing a degree of order and control. He is required to ensure that no one on his beat violates any of the hundreds and hundreds of statutes that govern street behaviour and to report any illegal or suspicious activities or persons. His presence is supposed to act as a deterrent to potential offenders. The populace, on its part, is supposed to cooperate with the police in maintaining law and order, raise alarms and earn awards. But, obviously, this is not how it works out.

A situation where laws, judicial directives, and government

policy render an entire way of living illegal poses serious problems for even the doughtiest of constables. The constable and the denizens are then confronted with a choice—to either embark on a determined and foolhardy drive to wipe out every trace of illegality that sullies the fair face of the capital, and finally results in a riot, a lathi-charge, and bad press all around, or to work out a strategy of mutual respect, support and understanding where both parties arrive at a mutually beneficial interpretation of the rules accompanied by ritualistic face-saving for all.

The pact between the constable and the workers, shopkeepers and interlopers at Bara Tooti is based on the axiomatic truth that everyone has a family to feed—hence any compromise that hampers the job prospects of either the constable or the denizens is bound to fail. Thus the constable approaches his daily duties with a certain reluctance to act unless a transgression becomes impossible to ignore. The denizens on their part ensure that they never openly flout a constable's authority. As Mohamed Ashraf, a worker at Bara Tooti told me, '*Yahan jo bhi karna hai karo, bus khullam khulle mein mat karo.*' 'Khullam khulla'—literally, 'out in the open', is a popular phrase that conveys an openness so brazen and complete that it borders on excess. Popular usages include 'khullam khulla *pyaar karenge*'—made more popular by a Bollywood box-office disaster of the same name, starring Govinda and Preity Zinta—that speak of a love that is so great and fearless that it cannot be hidden, and 'khullam khulla loot', which is usually used to describe particularly shameless corruption among the rank and file of the state.

In the classic compact between the police and the *janta*, the khullam khulla violation of laws—like playing cards, drinking alcohol, selling marijuana or simply sleeping on the pavement in full public view qualifies as the extenuating circumstances that warrant a police crackdown. After all, if the constable does not act when the writ of the law is violated khullam khulla, he runs the risk of losing his job when the deputy commissioner of police drops in for a surprise inspection.

Thus, business is conducted *chupke chupke,* the name of a far more popular Bollywood film starring Amitabh Bachchan, Dharmender, Jaya Bachchan and Sharmila Tagore, among others. By postulating that suspicious transactions be conducted in narrow *gallis*, darkened shops and away from the main road, the 'chupke chupke' formulation works on the premise that given the opportunity, the police will look the other way.

Lalaji's tea shop in Barna Galli, Bara Tooti is a good example of how this formulation works. From a distance, Lalaji's doesn't look so much like a shop as it does the fossilized remains of a creature formed by the successive spawning of entire generations of pots, pans, stoves and cement. On closer inspection, it proves to be a large concrete shelf—about six feet high, ten feet across and three feet deep—that had been fused onto the rear wall of the Aggarwal Samiti Mandir premises. The mandir management has leased out half the shelf to a machinist, who spends his day crouched on his narrow ledge with an array of lathes, wires, capacitors and resistors for company. The other half had originally been rented out to a jeweller, but that shop had long packed up and the mandir and the jeweller are now engaged in an acrimonious legal battle for possession of the space. Sanjay 'Lalaji' Kumar, the cheerful, chatty proprietor of the Barna Galli tea shop sub-leased the shop from the jeweller five years ago, and has dutifully deposited his rent of 200 rupees every month in court ever since.

Lalaji's shop is illegal for several reasons—it is a commercial establishment without a licence, it does not follow most laws set out to regulate eating houses and it is an illegal add-on to a quasi-legal construction. But that doesn't seem to bother Lalaji. His shop is in the inner part of the inner part of Barna Galli—insulated from even the nosiest of DCPs. Of course the local constable knows it exists—it is, after all, his job to know—but occasionally, certain sums of money exchange hands, and the shop continues to run as it has for the five years since its inception. Lalaji's uncle also happens to be the local BJP councillor, and Lalaji makes no attempts to conceal the fact. However, Lalaji also knows that if he had set up shop in the centre of the chowk, the police would be forced to act—and no political connections would be able to save him.

Munna Lal's case, by contrast, illustrates how not to deal with the police force at Bara Tooti. A few months ago, Munna made the crucial error of getting into a drunken brawl on the main road. Unsurprisingly, a constable arrived within minutes. Refusing to slip away into the anonymous gallis, Munna chose instead to enquire about the constable's sexual prowess. A lathi swung through the air, and broke both of Munna's arms.

However, it would be simplistic to view the relationship between the constable and the inhabitants of the chowk as purely extortionist. There is no doubt that the constable does wield a considerable amount of power, and that life at the chowk is kept at an even keel as long as his power is continually acknowledged. However, the constable too is vulnerable to the chowk in subtle ways that aren't always apparent or intelligible to the disinterested passerby. The most obvious vulnerability of the constable is the fact that everyone at the chowk knows exactly how little his monthly salary is, and most shopkeepers at the market are in a position to augment it. The dictum that everyone has a family to feed, spares no one—not even the constable.

Hence, in a traditional constable-led surveillance scenario, the chupke chupke formula works by placing illegality just beyond the line of sight of the constable—allowing him the option of 'not seeing'. Acts committed khullam khulla break the compact between police and the janta and force the constable to act.

*

DCP A.K. Garg's office is far removed from the dusty market that is the workplace of the constable at Bara Tooti. Designated DCP-North, Garg is in charge of all police operations conducted in the North Zone and sits in a plush office near the Vidhan Sabha. However, modern technology has ensured that the world of DCP Garg and his constables are no longer as far apart as they once were. Ten days ago, the friendly man from the computer department installed a sleek new Dell machine on DCP Garg's table. Now, DCP Garg can surf the Net, send e-mail, and make new friends on Orkut at a mere click of the mouse; but most importantly, he can keep tabs on the entire North Zone through a series of twenty-five high-resolution, fully manoeuvrable digital cameras that stream live footage to his desktop twenty-four hours a day, seven days a week.

According to an employee of Turbo, the company tasked with providing the hardware and software solutions for the project, 'The cameras installed across Delhi are (wouldn't you know it) truly world-class. Each camera has a 12x optical zoom capability, a special high-contrast night mode, and is equipped to take still photographs. All cameras are connected to a massive intranet that has been set up especially for the Delhi Police by Airtel—the telecom wing of Bharti Enterprises, and carry unique I.P. addresses. The support infrastructure for the intranet is physically separated from that provided by Airtel for its commercial internet consumers to minimize security risks, and each set of cameras is connected to a battery of eight serially connected 400 GB hard drives, giving the system a combined storage capacity of 4.3 terabytes.' And, if the Turbo employee is to be believed, 'This is just the beginning.'

By virtue of its location in the heart of DCP Garg's domain, the chowk at Bara Tooti has also been fitted out with its very own surveillance cameras that allow the DCP to keep track of the street from the comfort of his office. The cameras were installed in early 2004 after the police intercepted an explosives-laden truck, believed to be operated by the Jaish-e-Mohammed, in the parking lot on nearby Qutb Road. Since then, the police claim that the cameras have helped them track down several suspicious persons and most recently helped catch individuals involved in a robbery in Sadar Bazaar that left a shop-owner poorer by almost six lakh rupees.

While senior police officers can't stop raving about the efficacy of the cameras, the eye in the sky has created a few problems for our local constable. Apart from the DCP's office, the camera feeds are beamed to the nearest police thana—the Sadar Thana in the case of Bara Tooti—which usually lies in a one-kilometre radius. However, the constable on duty has no access to the feed; he relies on instructions passed on to him from his seniors via wireless. Thus, a surveillance operator in the local thana scans the length and breadth of a particular area for suspicious persons, objects and actions, and then asks the constable on the ground to investigate. The camera itself is incapable of making distinctions or decisions, and so the constable remains the most immediate part of the surveillance: the verification apparatus. While the untiring eye of the camera does not decide on action, it is very effective in raising suspicion. The bleached, slightly grainy images captured by the camera make everyone look like a potential threat, and the absence of an audio feed gives everything a grim, slightly sinister air. The presence of the camera forces the constable to acknowledge that he too is constantly under supervision, and this alters the nature of the alliance between the residents and the constable. When interviewed, senior police officers directly involved in the project spoke glowingly of how the surveillance camera shall bring greater accountability to all levels of the police force, 'particularly among the subordinate ranks'. It is useful to note that, in this context, the increased accountability of the policeman refers to his accountability to his superiors, not necessarily to the residents on his beat.

A camera in the main chowk leads to subtle shifts in the nature of the interaction between power and her subjects. While those tucked away in side alleys still escape the glare of the lens, those on the main road have to evolve newer forms of camouflage. The possibility of increased monitoring forces the policeman to be more thorough with his checking than he, or the residents, would like him to be, with a detrimental effect on the carefully arranged locus of the street. The constable's new job profile as the verifier of the camera does not allow him to 'not see' certain things because the camera sees everything. Thus, the chupke

chupke code takes a serious beating in these circumstances because anything that looks even slightly furtive is an advertisement for further investigation. If asked to check whether an unattended bag on the street (that shows up on the screen at the monitoring station) contains any bomb-making paraphernalia—a constable cannot say, 'No, it only has a few pouches of marijuana.' Instead, he has to report his findings, be commended for his role in a drug bust, and earn the wrath of the local marijuana peddler who pays him a few hundred rupees a month specifically to look the other way.

Instead, one sees the beginnings of what could be called the Khullam Khulla Inversion. The Khullam Khulla Inversion works on the principle that in a scenario of constant supervision, complete visibility is often the best camouflage. In fact, one can stretch the metaphor further, by suggesting that certain processes can often be rendered so transparent that that they become invisible.

In his *Art and Camouflage: An Annotated Biblography of Camouflage*, Roy Brehan lists different techniques of camouflage—one of them being Mimetic Resemblance. Mimetic resemblance is a form of camouflage that does not seek to hide an object, but merely makes it look like another object that is of little interest to the seeker. The Khullam Khulla Inversion works as a form of urban mimetic resemblance which preys on the assumption that no one breaks laws in broad daylight. What is furtive is immediately suspect, but that which is done out in the open is usually let pass.

The Khullam Khulla Inversion also explains how it is easier to drink on the streets by day, than by night. In the harsh sunlight of the afternoon, the group of workers drinking their way to amusement appear a cheerful bunch of young men sharing chai. The steel tumblers in their hands appear innocuous and non-threatening. The empty bottle of Pepsi by their feet is just an example of the poor civic sense endemic to the denizens of this fair city. Everything is done khullam khulla; everyone is happy and rapidly getting happier. By night, the same space is transformed into a den of vice and debauchery. The surveillance camera switches to high-contrast mode, and the group of workers transforms into devious outsiders plotting the overthrow of the state. The innocent steel glasses of the afternoon are now opaque tumblers of the twilight, specifically chosen to conceal their contents. The empty bottle of Pepsi is now taken as evidence of an attempt to mask the smell and colour of cheap whisky, and before you know it, a constable has been dispatched to break up the merry gathering.

The Khullam Khulla Inversion works simply because no one expects it to. It also explains why so many things that are patently obvious at the level of the street—like a bottle of whisky lying next to a worker's tools or the thick scent of marijuana emanating from a worker's beedi—pass through the scanner without a murmur, while other seemingly sinless objects—like a wheelbarrow left unattended on the road—are picked up. It is because the camera is no longer looking for them specifically. The camera is trained to look for the two things that annoy the middle classes—traffic congestion and terrorist conspiracies. Anything else that gets picked up en route is just collateral.

At the International Trade Fair 2006, the Delhi Police set up an attractive and interactive road-safety stall in an attempt to bring the wonders of surveillance closer to the public. Inspector Nandal, the chief organizer, encouraged attendees to use the cameras themselves and walked members of the press through a model street layout—complete with peizo-electric speed sensors, surveillance cameras, and self-regulating traffic lights. A reporter pointed at a small speaker installed under each light. 'Is the speaker to warn the public to follow traffic rules?' the young man asked the good inspector.

'Oh no, no,' he replied. 'Studies have shown that traffic rules are usually broken by stressed and tense commuters. The speakers are designed to play light, soothing music to calm harried commuters at rush hour.'

Father-in-law Has Pots of Money

AVIJIT GHOSH

When film star Rani is mobbed in the hinterlands of Uttar Pradesh and Bihar, the surname is not always Mukherjee. Just as Ms Mukherjee rules Bollywood, Rani Chatterjee is an icon in Bhojpuri filmdom. In the difference in the fame and fortune of the two Ranis lies the untold story of two disparate worlds: India Shining and India Invisible.

When the Bhojpuri film *Sasura Bada Paisewala* (Father-in-law Has Pots of Money) was released in May 2004, few in Bollywood took notice. The absence of enthusiasm was understandable—Bhojpuri cinema had shown little art or enterprise. While, after its gallant birth in the early '60s, the regional genre had enjoyed a boom in the late '70s and early '80s, in the new millennium, it went into a kind of coma. 'Give up,' the Hindi film industry seemed to whisper into its ear as it lay dying.

Then the unthinkable happened. At a time when 90 per cent of mainstream Hindi films were dying like flies at the box-office, *Sasura Bada Paisewala*'s rustic tale of a young man's battle for self-respect against a rich and scheming father-in-law touched a hidden chord in the hearts of Bhojpuri movie maniacs. The comatose had suddenly burst into life.

Sasura... brought the word 'jubilee' back into the regional film trade. The dusty golden jubilee boards were cleaned, polished and hung outside the halls as the film completed fifty weeks in Varanasi. In four other Uttar Pradesh towns—Gorakhpur, Deoria,

Kanpur and Lucknow—the movie ran to packed houses for over twenty-five weeks. 'No film had celebrated a silver jubilee in the history of Deoria before,' the film's co-producer Sudhakar Pandey told me with evident satisfaction. In Bihar too, the film wowed the cash counter, reaching the silver jubilee mark in little-known Hajipur.

The tin-roofed cinema halls of mofussil towns, where men often strip down to their underwear during the summer matinee shows, were full to capacity. The long queues before the ticket counters reminded old-timers of another movie: *Jai Santoshi Ma*, the freak 1975 super hit. The film, made on a shoestring Rs 30 lakh, ended up grossing Rs 9 crore, possibly more. No Hindi film could boast of a higher percentage of profit in 2004. Simply put, *Sasura Bada Paisewala* was the *Sholay* of Bhojpuri films.

Few know, though, that the making of the movie itself was a miracle. Two days before shooting commenced in November 2003, director Ajay Sinha began vomiting blood. Years later, Sinha still isn't exactly sure why. 'Maybe I had chewed a shard of glass with my tandoori roti,' he ventures. The effect of his unlikely ailment was damaging.

The director was immediately admitted to a Gorakhpur hospital. 'The doctor told me two things: "Take rest and don't talk,"' the director recalls. Sinha hadn't heard a more depressing sentence in his life.

The unit had already reached its outdoor location, Shamshabad village in the adjoining Mau district. And everyone was waiting for the cameras to roll.

For debutant co-producer Pandey, calamity had struck. He had to make a choice: either go ahead with the schedule or cancel the shoot. 'If I had taken the unit back,' says Pandey, reconstructing those tension-filled days, 'the film might have never been made.' Finally after much deliberation, he took the choreographer's advice to shoot the songs first.

On his part, Sinha, a science graduate from Magadh University, was determined to direct the film. 'I told the doctor, "I have nothing more to lose than my life and this film",' he recalls. Contrary to the doctor's advice, he left the hospital within a few days and joined the unit. Initially, he wrote out his suggestions on a piece of paper. Obviously, that wasn't enough. As a director, he needed to give orders. Since he was also playing the role of an aggressive *sasur*, he needed to shout out his lines. He would still bleed occasionally from the mouth, but Sinha stuck to his job. 'Despite the risk, I did not hesitate to scream at the top of my lungs,' he says.

The shooting was completed in a mere twenty days. Hero Manoj Tiwari, a successful folk singer of *kajris, chaitas* and *purabiyas* from Varanasi, got Rs 2 lakh for the film. Now he is said to charge Rs 40 lakh. *Sasura...* was ready for viewing by March 2004.

Unfortunately, politics intervened. With the Lok Sabha elections set to be held in April and May, Pandey felt the release should be postponed. 'In Uttar Pradesh and Bihar, elections are like festivals. Everyone is involved. So I decided to advance the date,' says Pandey, a former customs trading agent. The decision was also prompted by the lukewarm feedback garnered from the film's sneak previews. One distributor from Gorakhpur wanted to be generous with his praise. 'It will run at least for a week,' he said. The sceptics were proved wrong. But the trade pundits were unwilling to accept *Sasura*'s success as anything more than a fluke. One swallow does not make a summer, they said.

The second swallow arrived with *Panditji Batai Na Biyaah Kab Hoi* in 2005. The film starred Ravi Kissen, the son of a Jaunpur priest and a graduate from Benaras Hindu University. Till then, Kissen had survived in Bollywood's backwaters doing bit parts in movies such as Salman Khan's *Tere Naam*. The film's heroine Naghma had stayed alive in north Indian memory more for her alleged romance with then India cricket captain Sourav Ganguly than her movies. 'But she was still a well-known star down south. And I had to literally plead with her to do a Bhojpuri film,' recalls Kissen.

Nobody was interested, though. To create some buzz around the movie, Kissen hit upon an idea. Borrowing inspiration from Marilyn Monroe's famous red skirt-flying scene in *The Seven Year Itch*—also redone by Kelly Le Brock in *The Woman in Red* and Pooja Bedi in *Jo Jeeta Woh Sikander*—he conjured up a similar scene through the song, '*Lehnga utha deb remote se*' (I will lift your skirt through a remote.) 'The gimmick attracted the media and created a much-needed hype about the film,' says Kissen, now a well-known star whose smart-talk performance in the Sony reality TV show, *Bigg Boss*, widened his mass appeal. His foam-soaked face in another reality TV show, *Bathroom Singer*, now adorns hundreds of huge banners in metros.

The unlikely Kissen-Naghma on-screen partnership stormed the box office. Industry sources say that the film, made for Rs 60 lakh, ended up grossing at least ten times more. In Patna alone, the film collected more than four times the amount the mainstream rage *Bunty aur Babli* (Shaad Ali's movie about small-town yearnings) pulled in. 'With *Panditji...*, we hit the jackpot,' says Kissen.[1]

---

[1]Quoted from 'Enter Bhollywood: Bhojpuri potboilers back with a bang' (*The Times of India*, 1 July 2005)

Mainstream Hindi film industry was stunned. A second superhit, even from the boondocks of central India, was hard to ignore. Suddenly, Bhojpuri cinema was hot and happening. What followed was the great Bhojpuri rush. For dozens of small producers, directors, distributors and actors, the genre became the potential golden goose. 'Some producers who didn't even know the ABC of Bhojpuri culture wanted to cash in on the craze,' says *Panditji*'s director Mohanji Prasad. Even in the halcyon late '70s, when films like *Dangal* and *Balam Pardesiya* became superhits, the genre was never in such great demand. Delhi-based distributor Sanjay Mehta summed up the scenario aptly. He called it 'the Laloo phenomenon of cinema'.[2]

---

[2]Quoted from Namrata Joshi's article, 'Ab hamar film hit hoi', in *Outlook* magazine (3 October 2005)

Since then, the genre's upward social mobility was rapid. Who would have ever forecast that Amitabh Bachchan (*Ganga*), Ajay Devgan (*Dharti Kahe Pukar Ke*), Hema Malini (*Ganga*) would act in Bhojpuri films? That thespian Dilip Kumar would produce a film (*Ab To Ban Ja Sajanwa Hamaar)* in the regional dialect? That the genre would provide succour and employment to ex-Miss Worlds such as Yukta Mookhey who forked out an item for *Kab Kehba Tu I Love You*? That these films would be shot abroad (*Kab Hoi Gauna Hamaar*) and even attract *firang*

heroines? And who in his devilish dreams would have foreseen six prints of *Spiderman 3* being dubbed in Bhojpuri—and Kissen being the *desi* voice of Toby Maguire?

Now everybody wants a slice of the regional cinema's growing market pie. Even satellite television channels, Star Gold and Sahara, started showing 'Bhojwood' movies regularly. In early 2007, Star acquired the rights for thirteen films, including superstar Manoj Tiwary's hit *Daroga Babu I Love You*. The genre's expanding market can be gauged by the fact that weekly trade magazines such as *Film Information* now carry film reviews of Bhojpuri movies too. Every issue carries production reports of films in the making. Industry sources estimate Bhojpuri cinema to be worth Rs 100 crore. It caters to about 200 million people and offers employment to around 30,000. The genre's fast-expanding market can also be gauged from the fact that Ekta Kapoor's Balaji Telefilms' *Gabbar Singh* was dubbed in Telugu, Tamil and Kannada.

Bhojpuri films also have a huge potential audience in the diaspora. Back in the late nineteenth and early twentieth century, thousands of Indians from Bihar and eastern Uttar Pradesh were shipped off to different parts of the globe to work in sugarcane plantations. Now in countries like Mauritius, Fiji, Guyana and Trinidad, they form the Bhojpuri-speaking diaspora. At least in Mauritius and Fiji, they still speak the language and croon folk songs that have filtered orally down the generations. Many of these people have migrated again to countries such as the US and Canada. If tapped properly, pundits believe, this dollar-rich diaspora wouldn't mind investing in Bhojpuri VCDs and DVDs.

Dinesh Lal Yadav, better known by his pet name Nirahua, now forms, along with Tiwary and Kissen, the holy trinity of male stardom in Bhojpuri films. A fine folk singer of *birha*s, Nirahua's successes include the 2007 superhit *Nirahua Rickshawala*. One can see shades of Rajnikant in his fight scenes. And much like Bollywood's 'Kissinger' Emraan Hashmi, Nirahua too isn't shy of kissing heroines. Like any Bollywood filmstar, Nirahua recently conducted stage shows in Fiji, Australia and New Zealand. He is set for twenty shows in USA and Canada.

In other words, the new Bhojpuri star is no longer satisfied being a lowbrow, small-time player. He wants a share of the dollar first-world.

But actors like Nirahua, Tiwari and Kissen owe much of their success to the commitment of the early dreamers who laid the foundation of the industry. Central Board of Film Certification statistics show that between the years 1962-95, 145 Bhojpuri films were made. In 1986 alone, the number reached a record nineteen.

It started off in 1962 with *Ganga Maiya Tohe Piyari Chaddaibo* (O Mother Ganga, I Will Offer You the Yellow Cloth), the first Bhojpuri feature. The story goes that the film's scriptwriter Nazir Hussain, whom old-timers might recall as the benevolent Christian priest who brings up Anthony (Amitabh Bachchan) in Manmohan Desai's *Amar, Akbar, Anthony*, met India's first president Dr Rajendra Prasad and discussed his plans to make a film on the Central Indian dialect. 'It is a great idea,' said the President who went to school in the Bhojpuri-speaking district of Chhapra. But, he added: 'To execute the idea, you would need a lot of hard work and courage. If you possess these features, go ahead and make the movie.'

The black-and-white film premiered in Varanasi's Prakash Talkies. *Ganga Maiya...* was the story of a young widow's predicament, with Kumkum turning out as the leading lady. And they didn't dare make even a Bhojpuri film without Helen those days. Made for Rs 5 lakh, the movie grossed many times over. Film historian Firoze Rangoonwala writes, 'Directed by Kundan Kumar, the film was a typical romantic melodrama, but the novelty of its language and folk music made it such a sensational hit that it let loose a flood of films in its sister dialects.'[3]

*

Indeed, Chitragupta's music was the film's real strength. Born in Bihar's Gopalganj district, the music director was a post-graduate in economics. Few Bollywood composers could infuse the smell and flavour of rural central India with as much elegance as he. Apart from the hummable title track, he gave two timeless compositions for the movie.

'*Sonva ke Pinjra Mein*' (In the Golden Cage) can easily find a place among the 100 best sad songs sung by Mohammed Rafi. Till the '80s, this hauntingly heart-breaking track was often heard on Vividh Bharati along with Lata Mangeshkar's *Kahe Bansuriya Bajaule* (Why Did You Play the Flute?).

Despite the super success of *Ganga Maiyya*, the growth of Bhojpuri films was more steady than spectacular. In the following year, two more movies were released: *Bidesiya*, with Sujit Kumar, the well-known character actor of the '70s and '80s, in the lead role. Bhikari Thakur, the poet and actor who shaped Bhojpuri

---

[3]Quoted from *A Pictorial History of Indian Cinema*, by Firoze Rangoonwala, Page 92, Hamlyn, 1979.

folk theatre, also acted in the film. *Lagi Nahin Chhoote Rama* was the second offering from the *Ganga Maiyya* team. The movie had a great duet by Talat Mehmood and Lata Mangeshkar: '*Lali Lali Oonthwa Se, Barse ho Lalaiya ho ke Ras Choowela*' (Your Red Lips Drip Nectar).

But the regional film went through a slump in the early '70s. Between the years 1969 and 1977, only one Bhojpuri flick was released.

The genre's second coming was primarily spurred by two films. The first, *Dangal* (1977) will be remembered as the top music director pair of the Nineties, Nadeem-Shravan's debut film. '*Kashi hile, Patna hile*'—a take-off on the original folk number, '*Arrah hile, Chhapra hile*'—was the chartbuster of the year. Character actor Sujit Kumar and beauty queen-bit-actress Prema Narayan played the lead pair. Then, *Balam Pardesiya* (1978), directed by Nazir Hussain, became a whopper of a hit. The film turned flop hero Rakesh Pandey and '70s item girl Padma Khanna into regional superstars. Chitragupta's folksy tunes ('*Gorki Patarki Re*' and '*Hanse jo Dekhe tu Ek Bariya*') again spurred its success.

But none of these films altered the matrix of popular cinema in Bihar and eastern UP. Back in the '70s, Bhojpuri film was still an exception to the Bollywood rule. But in the post-*Sasura* and *Panditji* world order, the changes are deeper and much more far-reaching. These days Bhojpuri cinema has really overtaken mainstream Bollywood in the smaller towns of the region. If there are three cinema halls in a town, chances are two of them will be showing Bhojpuri films. This was not the case in the '70s. The sheer quantum of films being produced in the regional genre is huge now. As per industry estimates, at least 80 Bhojpuri films have been released since *Sasura...* hit the silver screen in 2004.

But the real reason behind the rise of Bhojpuri cinema lies in mainstream Bollywood cinema's own paradigm shift. Since 1931, when *Alam Ara* was released, Mumbai cinema was primarily a cinema of mass sensibility. An Amitabh Bachchan-starrer such as *Ganga Ki Saugandh* or *Mr Natwarlal* reached out to urban, small-town and rural audiences alike. No longer. In the past few years, with the rise of a rich middle class and the elevation of the NRI circuit abroad, most new Bollywood film-makers believe that it is possible to bypass middle India. The multiplexes, with their high-priced tickets, have given them the opportunity to make films that suit the tastes and the sensibilities of this class. The phenomenon has caused an explosion of feel-good cinema where the village, the ageing and the underprivileged have been all but eased out of the frame.

Part of Bhojpuri cinema's rise is a reaction to such a state of affairs. The audience seems to be telling mainstream Bollywood: if you ignore us, we will ignore you. What happened to north Indian politics after the Mandal Commission recommendation was implemented has now happened in the entertainment industry. As in politics, the entertainment industry too has stratified. Forget what is good or bad; the issue is this: I need my own cinema, that suits my own aesthetics.[4]

To its audience, the Bhojpuri films are the artistic equivalent of Grandmother's pickles. Watching a film like *Damadji* in Old Delhi's Chandni Chowk area, it is easy to understand why these

---

[4] This argument first appeared in my article, 'The mofussil's revenge', (*The Times of India*, 1 November 2005).

films work. For the thousands of migrant labourers from eastern UP and Bihar spread across north India, these films are about memories, yearnings and sharedness. For a few hours, the auditorium becomes their home away from home. Watching the movie is a way of keeping in touch with the folks back there.

The success of these films is also indicative of the levels of migration that have taken place. In the past two decades, millions have migrated from these two states to different parts of the country. Maharashtra, Punjab, Rajasthan and the national capital region of Delhi, which includes satellite towns such as Ghaziabad, Noida and Gurgaon, all have substantial Bihari and eastern UP populations. The film genre's presence outside its core geographical area is rooted in this social trend.

Joginder Mahajan, a Bhojpuri film distributor in Delhi and Uttar Pradesh, says that two decades ago, even a superhit like *Balam Pardesiya* ran only in morning shows in the national capital. On the contrary, *Sasura Bada Paisewala* was shown in ten cinema halls for a record five prints. It ran for twelve weeks in Sangam near UP's Loni border; more than any Shah Rukh, Salman or Aamir movie. Interestingly, most Bhojpuri films are shown in areas with a huge migrant labour population. In Moti at Old Delhi's Chandni Chowk, the cinema hall attracts the cart-pullers and rickshaw-wallahs, all of whom work in the Kashmere Gate, Chawri Bazaar, Sadar Bazaar and Khari Baoli business areas. In December 2006, a Bhojpuri film was released for the first time in Jaipur. *Panditji Batain* did quite well even in Punjab and Mumbai, thanks again to a huge migrant population.

There's obviously a message in all this. The Bhojpuri films' success is actually a form of protest. It is a slap on the cheek of arrogance that believes it is possible to sell anything to those who don't have a choice. The industry's re-emergence shows that even in the worst of situations, ignored voices always find ways and means of being heard.

Notes on Contributors

Nirupama Dutt is a journalist of many seasons, having worked with *The Indian Express* at Chandigarh and Delhi for most of her career. She has written extensively on Punjab as a journalist and as an author. Her published books include a collection of poems—*Ik Nadi Sanwali Jahi* (A Stream Somewhat Dark)—and several anthologies, in English translation, of Hindi and Punjabi poetry and short fiction. At present she is working as Punjabi Editor for *The Sunday Indian* at Chandigarh.

Avijit Ghosh grew up in the small town of Arrah in Bihar's fertile Bhojpur district. As a teenage film addict, he was initiated into the world of Bhojpuri films back in 1978 when he watched the noon show of *Balam Pardesiya* in the Moti Mahal cinema hall. He hasn't stopped watching them since. Now a journalist with *The Times of India*, he is working on a book on Bhojpuri cinema.

Shubhra Gupta has been reviewing movies for the *Indian Express* for over sixteen years; for her writing about cinema is not drudgery, but a passion.

Gupta grew up watching Bombay masala in dusty UP cinema halls, bunked many Eng. Lit. undergrad classes to take in world cinema at Delhi University's Celluloid Society, and went on to study film formally at Sophia College, Bombay.

After some years in straight-up journalism as sub-editor and reporter at the *Hindustan Times* and *Sunday Mail*, she began a weekly TV review column which started in 1988 at the *Indian Post*, and then travelled to *Sunday*, till the end of the '90s.

The weekly movie column at the *Indian Express* began in 1992. Single-channel India was poised to turn into a 200-channel satellite dish. A few years after that, Bombay became Mumbai. And a media boom began, which has shown no signs of slowing down. Like everywhere else, TV and film have fed off each other: when it began, programming on TV was all film-based, then films began imitating TV, and now everybody happily copies everybody.

And Bollywood is cool, cool, cool.

Ashok Malik is senior editor with *The Pioneer*. A political journalist for the past 16 years, he has previously worked with a host of leading publications, including *India Today* and *Indian Express*. He lives in New Delhi with his wife and son.

Aman Sethi is a reporter for *Frontline* Magazine where he covers environment, infrastructure and urban ecologies. The 'Khullam Khulla Inversion' was first presented as a full length paper at the Sensor: Census: Censor conference at CSDS: Sarai in December 2006, and was based on his research as an Independent Fellow 2005-06 at Sarai.

Kriti Sharma moved from Rishi Valley School in Andhra Pradesh to Paris at the age of thirteen. She is currently doing her B.A. in International Affairs at the American University of Paris. She spent the last two summers working for NGOs in Senegal and India.

Shankar Sharma was born of Assamese descent inside Bellshill Maternity Hospital (now sadly defunct), Lanarkshire, Scotland, United Kingdom of Great Britain and Northern Ireland at 11:11 a.m. on Wednesday, 18 June, 1980. Since then it has all gone drastically downhill—and he has grown to despise Wednesday mornings. In the human race, Sharma came last and was twice nearly disqualified for false starts. He has however somehow managed to 'cut and paste' his way through the international media, working as a writer and journalist for various newspapers, magazines and websites in India, the Republic of Ireland, the U.A.E. (very briefly), and the U.K. (not briefly enough). He has subsequently abandoned that line in order to pursue a career in teaching history. He hopes to proselytize future generations towards his cause for global domination. One can only have deep sympathy with the kids.

Sankar Sridhar developed a head for heights early in life while climbing stairs, first to peddle pagers and then trousers, as a teenager in Calcutta. The regular exercise—skipping lunch, mounting steps and dashing down to outrun irate housewives—stood him in good stead when he finally swapped concrete staircases for the icy Himalayas.

After a few years of trekking and guiding tourists on trails in Sikkim, Darjeeling, and Kashmir, Sridhar, by then twenty, enrolled in a mountaineering course, and proceeded to earn his keep as an outdoor survival instructor in a Delhi-based adventure company.

Whether it was the effect of breathing rarified air for extended periods or a stroke of genius, he will never know, but one fine day, Sridhar tapped his fingers on the keyboard instead of feeling rock faces for holds and, in the process, found himself a toehold in journalism. His articles have appeared in *The Telegraph, The Statesman, The Times of India, DNA, India Today Travel Plus, Outlook Traveller, Swagat* and *DiscoverIndia*. His travels continue and photos from his escapades have been exhibited, published and won honours in national and international salons and contests.

Sridhar currently works for a media organization in Delhi, spending his spare time thinking of the role life will next throw at him.

Palden Gyalsten Tenzing left the Indian Administrative Service because he had better things to do. One of them was a motorbike run around the country, prompted by his wife throwing him out after he set up a hotel chain in Sikkim. He is currently licking his wounds somewhere in India. He is founder-member of the Vipassana Trust of Sikkim, runs a school for Buddhist monks and practises tai chi haltingly. He has been lead singer in a rock band and is friend to all. This chapter is from a work in progress with Penguin India.

Kishore Valicha has written poetry and short stories that have been published in *New Quest* and earlier in the *Writers' Workshop Miscellany*. His doctoral dissertation on Indian cinema, which later was published in book form, received a National Award from the Government of India. He has written two biographies for Penguin India on Ashok Kumar and Kishore Kumar.

in London and in an anthology of urban Indian writing to be published by the Italian imprint, *ISBN*.

Vijay Parthasarathy, 27, grew up in Bombay. Currently based in Madras, he writes for *The Hindu*.

Joan Pinto grew up in Bombay. She's been an engineer, copywriter and interior designer. Joan has written for a host of publications including *The Times of India, Femina, Design Today, India Today Travel, The CS Monitor*, Boston, and *Gulf News*. Her short fiction 'The Wretched and the Loved' appeared on *Long Story Short*, the e-zine, and a flash memoir 'The Scent of Sawdust' on *flashquake*. Her short story 'How Rifka Made Things Right' was published in *Favourite Stories for Girls* (Puffin).

When Joan is not writing she blows bubbles with her niece, studies the colours in people, runs an NGO, sips chai, hums off-key, wanders through graveyards, and travels. She can be contacted at huanita@yahoo.com or on www.joanpinto.wordpress.com.

Neel Kamal Puri was born in Ludhiana, Punjab, in 1956. She grew up in the erstwhile princely state of Patiala. Since 1979, she has worked as a lecturer in English Literature at different colleges in Patiala and Chandigarh. She is currently teaching Literature and Media Studies at the Government College for Girls, Chandigarh.

Nooreen Sarna is a sixteen-year-old student, a keen environmentalist and the winner of the Asian Age Poetry competition (August 2006).

Parismita Singh is currently working on a graphic novel.

passionate about the land she comes from; it has a way of creeping into almost all her works.

In 2005 she had won the Short Fiction contest hosted by Unisun Publishers and the British Council. The following year she won second prize in the Children's Fiction category of the same prize. In 2006, Jahnavi was also awarded a Charles Wallace Trust Fellowship to study Creative Writing in the UK. She lives in Bangalore.

Shakti Bhatt's award-winning short stories have appeared in journals and anthologies in India and the U.K. 'The Thief' won the 2005 Toto Funds the Arts Award for short fiction. Shakti was working on three novels when she died in early 2007. She was 26.

Uma Girish is an internationally published writer whose articles and features have been published in 7 countries. Uma's short fiction has won her several awards, the most recent being e-Author 7.0, India's Largest Online Talent Search. 'Voices Across Boundaries', 'Lunch Hour Stories', 'India Currents' and 'Espresso Fiction' are some of her fiction credits. She is also a Business English trainer and lives in Chennai with her husband and 14-year-old daughter.

Mridula Koshy makes her home in New Delhi. In the past she was a Union and Community Organizer in the United States but threw this over for the lucre and glamour of a career mothering her three. She has been published in the Canadian journal *Existere* and in the Zubaan Books anthology of new writing, titled *21 under 40*. Her work is also forthcoming in the English literary journal, *Wasafiri*, in an anthology of Indian stories published by Saqi press

Notes on Contributors

Temsula Ao has contributed a number of articles on oral tradition, folk songs, myths and cultural traditions of the Ao Nagas and linguistic diversities of the Naga tribes for journals like *Indian Literature* published by the Sahitya Akademi, *Indian Horizons: Journal of the Indian Council for Cultural Relations* etc. She is Professor in the department of English, North Eastern Hill University, Shillong and also Dean, School of Humanities and Education at NEHU. She was awarded the Padma Shri in 2007.

Tulsi Badrinath, born in 1967, lives in Chennai. She has a Bachelor's degree in English Literature and an MBA. Her poems and articles have appeared in various newspapers and journals. Her unpublished novel 'The Living God' has been longlisted for the Man Asian Literary Prize 2007. Tulsi learnt Bharatanatyam from a very young age and has performed widely in India and abroad. She quit her job as a manager in a bank to devote herself to dance and writing. Currently, she is working on a novel and a collection of short stories.

Jahnavi Barua trained as a doctor but is now a writer, a reader, a mother of a six-year-old and a wife, not necessarily in that order. She writes mainly short fiction. She writes because she cannot help it; she writes because she reads; she writes because she is otherwise largely speechless.

Jahnavi is from Assam in the North-East of India and is

FIRST PROOF

THE PENGUIN BOOK OF NEW WRITING FROM INDIA **3**

PENGUIN BOOKS

PENGUIN BOOKS
Penguin Books India Pvt. Ltd, 11 Community Centre, Panchsheel Park,
New Delhi 110 017, India
Penguin Group (USA) Inc., 375 Hudson Street, New York, New York 10014, USA
Penguin Group (Canada), 90 Eglinton Avenue East, Suite 700, Toronto, Ontario,
M4P 2Y3, Canada (a division of Pearson Penguin Canada Inc.)
Penguin Books Ltd, 80 Strand, London WC2R 0RL, England
Penguin Ireland, 25 St Stephen's Green, Dublin 2, Ireland
(a division of Penguin Books Ltd)
Penguin Group (Australia), 250 Camberwell Road, Camberwell,
Victoria 3124, Australia (a division of Pearson Australia Group Pty Ltd)
Penguin Group (NZ), 67 Apollo Drive, Rosedale, North Shore 0632, New Zealand
(a division of Pearson New Zealand Ltd)
Penguin Group (South Africa) (Pty) Ltd, 24 Sturdee Avenue, Rosebank,
Johannesburg 2196, South Africa

Penguin Books Ltd, Registered Offices: 80 Strand, London WC2R 0RL, England

First published by Penguin Books India 2007

Anthology copyright © Penguin Books India 2007
Copyright for individual pieces vests with the individual authors.
'The Thief' © Jeet Thayil. The story has appeared, in somewhat different form, in the
journal *New Quest*.

All rights reserved

10 9 8 7 6 5 4 3 2 1

ISBN-13: 978-0-14310-244-1   ISBN-10: 0-14310-244-3

Cover photograph and design by Pinaki De

Typeset in *Adobe Garamond* by SÜRYA, New Delhi
Printed at Pauls Press, New Delhi

Dedicated to the memory of Shakti Bhatt
who, sadly, didn't live to see her story published.

FICTION

Contents

Fiction

1 **Next Door**
JAHNAVI BARUA

4 **When the Child Was a Child**
MRIDULA KOSHY

19 **Strawberries**
KISHORE VALICHA

35 **Whorl**
VIJAY PARTHASARATHY

44 **Kailla**
NEEL KAMAL PURI

54 **The Lipstick**
UMA GIRISH

68 **The Saint of Lost Things**
JOAN PINTO

72 **An Offering**
TULSI BADRINATH

80 **The Floating Island**
PARISMITA SINGH

86 **The Thief**
SHAKTI BHATT

Poetry

105 **Nowhere Boatman**
         The Spear
         TEMSULA AO

111 **Bouquets**
         Mediterranean Siesta
         Refuge
         NOOREEN SARNA

113 **Notes on Contributors**

CONTRIBUTORS TO *FIRST PROOF*

VOLUME 1

Sarnath Banerjee * Ritu Bhatia * Alban Couto * Mamang Dai *
Rana Dasgupta * Mita Ghose * Indrajit Hazra * Ranjit Hoskote *
Arun John * Uma Mahadevan-Dasgupta * Palash Krishna Mehrotra *
Renuka Narayanan * Anuradha Roy * Mitali Saran * Navtej Sarna *
Ambarish Satwik * Paromita Vohra * André Béteille * Saba
Naqvi Bhaumik * Arpita Das * Sunanda K. Datta-Ray * Edna
Fernandes * Naresh Fernandes * Smita Gupta * Manmohan
Malhoutra * Jerry Pinto * Mishi Saran * Ajai Shukla * Nirupama
Subramanian * Sankarshan Thakur

VOLUME 2

C. Sriram * Sampurna Chattarji * Chandrahas Choudhury * Soumitro
Das * Sonia Faleiro * Dhruba Hazarika * K. Srilata * Rahul
Karmakar * Vivek Narayanan * E.V. Ramakrishnan * Anushka
Ravishankar * Satyajit Sarna * Manreet Sodhi Someshwar * Kanishk
Tharoor * Altaf Tyrewala * Annie Zaidi * Samrat Choudhury *
Dilip D'Souza * Salman Haidar * Manju Kak * Smriti Nevatia *
Sheela Reddy * Ranjana Sengupta * Pepita Seth * Arunava Sinha *
Sanjay Suri * Jeet Thayil

Next Door

JAHNAVI BARUA

You think that with time they would have grown accustomed to it, but they never do. At least once, every day, your father says, with a laugh, We hardly need the television, do we, folks next door provide enough entertainment. And your mother. Your mother's face is frequently dark and brooding. Like a thundercloud heavy with rain. If only I had known then, she hisses, we would never have bought this house.

They are right, of course. From daybreak till long into the restless night, there is a clamour and tumult in the house next door that manages to find its way around the edges of the bamboo wall that separates the two properties.

You are tantalized by that barrier. It is high, stretching well over your head and it is strong. The bamboo strips are woven tight together. But there are chinks. And you know where all the chinks are. That wall draws you and your brother like honeybees to nectar. What lies beyond is unspeakably alluring, and made even more so by your mother's constant warnings to stay away from it. You are frequently at that wall, one eye plastered to a chink. You settle down to the waiting. You draw deep into the well of your patience. Very often you see nothing at all. Just a column of sunlight that falls on a whitewashed wall.

And then again, sometimes you are lucky. Like the time you and your brother saw Maya, the girl next door, bathing at the open well in the backyard. You did not see very much, for Maya had a piece of cloth wrapped like a sarong around her, but once, when she bent down to soap her toes the cloth parted. There before you was a length of thigh—firm, muscled and yet so soft. Brown skin that gleamed in the sunlight and the breath caught in your chest in a way it had never done before. You glanced at your brother then and he would not meet your eye. His face was flushed. He turned away into the house. You were amused, but then you were only twelve and Rana was eighteen.

Maya has a mother. Tengesi, you and Rana have christened her, The Sour One, for she is as sour as a baby mango in April. You—and everybody else—are woken up every morning by Tengesi's venomous screeches that slice their way through the early morning mist and enter your warm dreams.

Wake up, you lazy dogs, is how Tengesi usually starts. Out of bed, you pigs, she screeches at her children.

Go to hell, her son shouts back. Bitch.

Tengesi's reply is frenzied. How dare you, you worthless swine, how dare you talk to me like that? If your father were here he would teach you.

But he isn't here, is he? He left you, didn't he? The son is jubilant.

Soon after this, familiar kitchen sounds start up. Metallic sounds and sounds of liquid being poured as Maya makes tea. You imagine her hurrying. Sometimes when she is late you hear the slapping sound of flesh hitting flesh. You hardly ever hear Maya. A soft murmur, a whimpering cry is all that you have heard.

But last week, you heard her voice clearly. The son had come in late at night, it was past ten, drunk as usual. Immediately there followed a disturbance. Sounds of furniture crashing to the floor, metallic objects being flung against hard surfaces. Tengesi's cracked voice hurling curses at her son. The sounds of a scuffle. And clearly Maya's voice breaking through the din.

Let me go, Dada, I beg of you. Please. *Please.*

Tengesi was hysterical now. You dog, get away from her.

A hard smacking sound and a thud as something heavy hit the floor.

Your father had half-risen in his chair, but your mother was quickly by his side. Let it be, she said, it is of no use.

You looked at Rana. His knuckles were white on the edge of the table.

Next morning you overslept. The world was white with light and you were perplexed. As if something was missing. And then you had it. You hadn't heard Tengesi's morning invocations. You never hear Tengesi again. And no one ever speaks of it. Not even Rana.

Months pass by. It has been quiet. Tengesi is still silent and Maya has not appeared. You think that maybe the women have gone somewhere.

Then one day, recently, Rana and you are walking to the teashop at the corner. You have to cross the house next door to get there. As you pass you see a figure on the verandah. It is Maya. She sees you and turns away. You see her belly round as a giant grapefruit. Your ears are hot. You look at Rana. His face is tight and hard and his eyes scream at you. He walks briskly ahead.

3

When the Child Was a Child

MRIDULA KOSHY

From one Thanksgiving to the next, a father, a mother, a child, and her siblings lived together under one roof. Their home was an apartment and the 'roof' was really a ceiling coated in drips of stucco. The real roof punched up eight floors above their heads, and contained under it sixty units to house the residents of 1609 N. Normandie, between Sunset and Hollywood. And although the child thought of these other residents as families, even as an extension of her own family, they were really the left-over bits of what were once families—families fragmented by any number of great upheavals that had torn them apart and sent them from all parts, long distances, to 1609.

They were not the amputees but rather the amputated parts from surgery on a scale that required a 1609-sized waste dump. It is said that the amputee experiences the ghost presence of what is removed, even scratching at the space vacated by a severed limb. But neither is the absent limb immune to the twitching of sundered nerves. So there was old Mrs. Markham who woke the building, her terror spasmodic in nature, only on certain nights, to check that the building's electric stoves were not doing the impossible by gassing them all in their sleep. And directly above the child lived Short Hair who, when he wasn't vacuuming the floor side of her ceiling, wept into the nylon fur he cleaned— wept the loss of girlfriends, wept the coming-down-from-speed-sound, which the child listening below thought the sound of the vacuum bag now filling with pins. There was the childless couple—the Mudiamus—whom the child's mother told her to be nice to—*poor things they realized too late that all the years they day-and-night-managed the Dairy Queen should have been years they were making a child instead.* Being nice to the Mudiamus was not an unpleasant task; as easy as agreeing to bags of M&Ms, excursions to Griffith Park and Castaic Lake.

On Thanksgiving Day, in 1979, inside the apartment with its built-in bar with a Formica top curving out from a mirrored wall, the child swiveled on a chrome and brown vinyl bar-stool and studied the comings and goings of her family members in the mirror she faced. The child's name was Emma. That was the day her father came from far away where he had been living in a place called a Correctional Facility, which she knew from the enemies at school was also the place called Jail. He came home that day with boxes of Twinkies and Dingdongs, and a lap into which he pulled the children's mother. The children, exultant and uncomfortable, ringed the tussling parents, and in the mirror Emma observed the great satisfaction of the whole.

Emma remembers it as the year they ate fish every night. But she is corrected when she brings up the memory to her mother who says, 'No, we might have eaten fish once or twice, but we were too poor to cook like that very often.' Emma, grown-up won't allow corrections. She murmurs her memories the better to savor them alone. 'We ate fish and you fed us like we were still too little to feed ourselves. When we had fish you always fed us. You made balls mixing the rice and the fish and the yoghurt, and we all saw you had to hurry to make more in between putting the balls into our mouths. When you couldn't keep up, we were mean. We would each yell "mine" and confuse

5

the order of your feeding. When you had a ball in your hand again we would each say, "give me." Then you would scold us, you would, yelling and saying, "I made it for you; who else am I going to feed it to?" We laughed at you then. You called us names in Malayalam—"fisherwomen", "Tamilians", you called us, and "starvelings". We never understood then how bad those words were in your mind. But the way you said those words, we knew you were angry, and we stopped laughing.'

That year, Emma remembers, they ate vindaloo pork patted into flour: soft fat thick-intact on stringy meat, and the rind of each piece that started out tough between her teeth crackling to release oil so rich she wanted nothing more than to live in her mouth. There was a dry preparation of beef, fried dark, to which slivers of coconut clung; and chicken in creamy gravy with bones good for crunching open and sucking the marrow from till the sharp breaks in the crenulations within grated fine the surface of her greedy tongue.

Her mother does not answer with memories of her own. Emma continues: 'Ribbon cake, like French crepes. Do they really make ribbon cake in Kerala—some kind of Malayalee dish, right? Or did you make it up yourself? We had that for tea a lot. Why did you call it cake? We kept wishing for real cake. I wanted Duncan Hines yellow cake with the pudding in the mix. We didn't know then how good the ribbon cake was.'

'We ate bread,' her mother says.

Emma smiles, untroubled. 'Weber's bread in a blue and white plastic wrap. Snoopy on the wrap. A cartoon of Woodstock saying something to Snoopy. They kept changing the cartoon but Woodstock's words were always just scribbles. You think I'd forget something from that year?'

Emma had been a skinny child that year and fast on the playground and street. Mostly people saw a blur, or if they paid attention they saw a blur of chapped cheeks-lips, and grey knees-elbows. That year Emma's sunken eyes had bled black under her lower lids. Her teachers who noticed worried that she reminded them of something worrisome. But, they could not pin a finger on what it was they were worried by till flipping through old issues of National Geographic, seeing there similar eyes paired with swollen bellies they made a mental note to check on her home situation, a note promptly peeled loose and lost to them till the next day seeing her eyes, they again began worrying.

'I don't remember anything called ribbon cake,' her mother says. 'Maybe somebody else made it.'

'Once at school when the counselor asked me what we ate I told her that we ate bread. Dr. King, that was her name; she kept trying to find out what we ate with the bread, and finally I said, "nothing." Then she stopped asking and stared. That's how I knew that I had given her the wrong answer. I knew she was going to call you. Kids always know what adults are going to do. I always knew. I knew I was going to be in trouble at home that day. See,' says Emma brightly, 'I remember everything.'

'We were never hungry,' her mother says. 'Day-old bread was dirt cheap and much older than that it was even free.'

'I used to roll the bread into balls. It was such soft bread, so full of air. I would eat the outside first—the brown part. Then I would roll up the middle and make balls and dip it into the fish curry. That was good.'

Her mother stares blankly at Emma. 'I don't remember making fish. Maybe once for your birthday.'

Emma had been taught that year—*turned ten is time to learn*

7

responsibility—to do the bread-run to the corner of Normandie and Hollywood. This same corner she encounters at twenty-three in screen images and newsprint words minting history, making her corner the corner where somebody else's story is unfolding. She leans forward to show her mother the pictures in the newspaper she holds out. 'That was a wonderful year.' Emma says. Emma is itching to read out loud the words in the paper but stops herself because she doesn't want to be mean to this old woman, whose hands are scuttling sideways over the front of her gown, plucking at the cloth for buttons that are not there. She covers her mother's hands with one of hers to stop their spider-legged run.

Her mother does not want to see the pictures. She loosens her hands from Emma's and turns away with difficulty; then defeated, turns back. Emma knows this is because the gown they have given her mother to wear must be unbearable to her with its gaping back and the strings she cannot reach to tie.

Her mother closes her eyes and tucks her chin deep into her chest. Some moments of silence follow. Then, not satisfied that she has effected a retreat, she again attempts the turn away from Emma, leaving behind just one arm to endure the struggle to pull up the bed sheet over her back. Emma gets up from her seat to offer assistance but is halted as the searching arm panics and thrashes blindly for the sheet end. She remembers the same hand, when younger, motioning to reach the sari end to draw it from the back to the front. Then, it had been a gesture to admire, a gesture of elegance. Emma covers her mother, though she longs instead to slap her.

Free to do so now that her mother has turned away, Emma makes hideous faces at the great white-sheeted mountain her mother laid on her side makes. Not satisfied with that, she makes karate-chop motions above the figure and jumps softly with each chop. The carpet underfoot absorbs the sound as it does the sound of the woman who enters from behind Emma. Emma pretends to be leaning over her mother, adjusting the sheets, but gives up when she realizes neither she nor the nurse really care what they each think of the other. This is the night-nurse coming to say her shift has ended. Before leaving she picks up the remote and switches off the screen which is endlessly replaying the images of Los Angeles burning that her mother had turned away from.

Emma is not sure if her mother is asleep or pretending to be. She talks to her mother's back: 'The time when Daddy came home on Thanksgiving you didn't know that he was coming, right? You didn't prepare. But the next year, I remember watching you cook.' That second Thanksgiving, the meal her father sprang from the table when he flipped the table onto her mother's lap—springing the legs from under her mother's chair, springing a fleck out of the youngest sibling's right cornea, springing 1979 free from the whole —had also sprung Emma's father from the family. 'You didn't want to make turkey. You thought maybe Daddy wouldn't like it to be so American. You made whole boiled eggs fried first so the skin was bubbled up the way I liked it. I should get a recipe book for Indian cooking and try it for myself.'

Soon after her father left, Emma's oldest sister followed, to keep house for her father. Then another sister left, to continue to keep to herself, but to do so even more convincingly by making her location unknown. The first sister came home to care for Emma and the younger siblings the one week, every three weeks, her mother worked the graveyard shift. When Emma asked her sister if she liked living with her father, her sister held to silence; moments passed and Emma, coming to know and feel her own stupidity, giggled. She was grateful when her sister giggled back with her. Her sister said, 'I will teach you to cook.' And once Emma learned, her sister no longer came; she was taken along when her father moved away.

For a long spell after Emma learned to cook she concentrated on perfecting the one recipe for which ingredients were usually available. She made what the younger siblings called 'Emma Pizza' by taking slices of Weber's bread, opening a can of tomato sauce, slathering the one with the other and by laying smooth over the whole a freshly-freed-from-plastic slice of cheese. These steps reminded her of nothing so much as making her bed. She was especially convinced of the similarity when the bread slices emerged from the checkered bag indented on two and sometimes all four sides, so that collapsed from the original square a bread slice was inadequate to the task of mating a whole cheese sheet. Her sister had advised cutting the extraneous bits of cheese and re-piecing them on another slice of bread to increase the count of 'Emma Pizza' at dinner. Emma discarded this economy, preferring to tuck all around, and folding down just on one side the extra cheese, as she folded down just on one side the top sheet of her bed. And when there was hotdog in the fridge she sliced it round and slipped a slice for a peeking-out face under this fold. Then she toasted her creation. Her cooking was good and her siblings told her so.

But the days there was no cheese and no sauce the siblings hated her, and to win them back Emma made tea and taught them to eat dipped-in-tea bread which they called 'Emma Tea

Cake.' While they dipped, she talked about the great meals they had eaten when their father had come to live with them. She talked about fish curry and rice, and chicken curry and rice, and beef curry and rice, and pork curry and rice. The siblings were too young to disbelieve her, although they could no longer remember who and what she was talking about. The nights they complained they were still hungry, she reminded them there would be eggs and hash browns at the school breakfast and spaghetti with taco meat for school lunch.

When all else failed, she launched them in a search for quarters under the washing machines lined up in the building basement. The search was suspended only when the furnace, asleep within a swirl of tentacled funnels, roared itself awake reminding them of the dead babies roasting within. Emma congratulated herself, as they fled upstairs, for having lucked into the perfect mix of hope and fear necessary to combat the boredom of their empty stomachs. On the occasion a stray quarter or two or three were found, the siblings headed to the bread corner, first racing past the dangers of the 'Mesican yard' filled with 'Mesican kids', then crossing the street, dodging the late evening Chevies, Buicks and Caddies exiting Sunset and turning the corner from Normandie to re-enter the parade cruising Hollywood.

Armed with found quarters, the bread corner became the Hubba Bubba corner. And when the younger siblings prevailed, their whining and moaning forcing her will to bend to theirs, then the Hubba Bubba Corner transformed itself into the Bubblicious corner. Down the street the younger ones swung, imitating the bounce-bounce of the agitated cars and trucks, too young to blow the proper bubbles, which Emma, who hung back strained her cheeks blowing.

Nights their mother came hurrying down the street toward them, home early from the late shift, gleaming white under the street lights, even from a distance shooing them inside, Emma pushed the younger ones in and stayed to witness the car windows rolling down to release the hooting and hollering heat within. Lingering, Emma saw the men in the cars push their heavy elbows out from the now open-to-the-dark interior and heard the drivers gunning and lurching and stopping their cars to mock her mother's gunning and lurching and stopping anger back at them. Then Emma scooted herself in before her mother reached home.

The day in December Emma's mother reached the 1609 street door and found Emma still standing there blowing Hubba Bubba in her mother's face, she grabbed Emma by the ear and dragged her in, all the while moaning, 'I don't care about the Fire Marshals. I'm locking you all in tomorrow when I leave. What kind of example are you to your sisters, Emma? Standing here in the doorway like some Mexican; teaching your sisters to be out on the street like the Mexicans.'

In the kitchen her mother brought out a bag of pink lentils and another of yellow and another of a different yellow and another of green. She settled distractedly on one of the colors, reached above the stove in the spice shelf and began quickly-tumbling to the counter bottles of whole chilies and mustard seeds.

'Did you cut and keep the onions and chillies and ginger like I asked you to?' Her mother washed her hands and started to wipe them on the front of her uniform, and then stopping herself, stripped in the kitchen; wiped her hands on the folds of her belly and turned to Emma, 'Did you put the rice to soak?'

'I fed them,' Emma said. And the siblings, their hunger chewed into the gum they were not supposed to, but had swallowed, nodded. 'We're not hungry. Emma fed us.' Then her mother cried and, sobbing, threw the cooking pots, clean and dry, into the sink and the younger ones went to bed.

That night her mother chopped onions, stirred and cooked in her pot something Emma, watching the simmer of anger, feared to eat. In the middle of the drama of siblings woken from sleep and dragged, heavy-eyed, to the table, Mrs. Markham set up her alarm. 'We're all going to die,' she wailed from the eighth floor, and wailing, swept down the stairs. At each floor she circled, pounding on the doors near the stairs. 'A conflagration,' she screamed, pointing her bony fingers up. Emma ran to the stairway, and peering up the steps spindled together and turning free from the ground, she saw clear to the glowing roof, and looking down, she saw a too-bright light in the lobby below. With her head wedged in the fourth sharp turn of the banister Emma called to her mother, 'Amma, Mrs. Markham's doing her crazy stuff again.' Through the open front door Emma heard in response the quiet misery of spoons moving in plates. Up and down the dim hallway, doors opened and emitted, 'Shut up,' and closed against Mrs. Markham's continued keening, which descended and descended till she was squatted with her nose pressed to Emma's, the smell from her mouth as she whimpered into Emma's face: foul. Emma heard, as if in a brief interlude, the licking sound of Mrs. Markham's long gown dissolving in small flames.

Then, from above Emma, people poured and poured out of their apartments, past her, down the stairs. And in the pouring of people and smoke she saw her mother—strange sight out of the house in her bra and slip—and sisters; she saw the youngest one turning her head hard around the one blind eye, searching for Emma. 'Emma,' her sister screamed and they swept past Emma who held still and heard the scratch in the voice of the man pulling at his wife, 'Honey, let's go back. There's still time for me to throw some stuff together. The fire's only on the eighth floor.' From below the voice of the building manager shouted into the din, 'Go back. Fire in the lobby. Head to the fire escapes.' And the crowd turned back up the stairs, and turned again on the sound of, 'locked.'

It was Short Hair who took the keys from the manager and raced heroically from floor to floor unlocking the fire escapes on each of the eight floors. Emma moved in a line of people that stepped over the ledge of the fourth floor's hallway window onto the black metal fire-stairs that crawled down the side of the building; and, hand over hand, in that line, she climbed down to the ground. There she found her mother and sisters and was forced with them across the street as they and the rest of the gathering crowd watched the firefighters go about their business.

Later that night, they were issued vouchers allowing them housing in the nearby motels. The stories circulated there were delicious. It was said that before the arrival of the firefighters, a mother in desperation had thrown her baby down from the eighth floor. But no one recalled a mother and baby living on the eighth floor. Emma played a bit-part in the storytelling; she described Mrs. Markham's nose crisping up right in front of her. After the fifth telling, even her sisters refused to hear more. It was known that the firefighters had transferred Mrs. Markham and Short Hair to County General. The speculation was that they would receive some sort of reward from the insurance company.

The firefighters made the decision, once all the residents were accounted for, to cease the effort to put out the fire. Instead, a limited team worked to contain it. It took eleven hours for the fire to burn itself out. The crowd outside the building melted into the dark of their own homes where they repeatedly woke in the night to check for faulty wiring and stoves left on. By that time the exhausted residents of 1609 were sprawled atop scratchy coverlets, asleep in strange beds, breathing in, in ragged rhythm, sooty sweat.

It took the firefighters five more days to move through the building and, floor by floor, clear the debris and declare each floor ready for the salvage crew, safe for eventual occupation. The haunted sleep of the building's residents and neighbors continued during those five days. Not until the firefighters came to a halt in the basement, where they discovered two charred bodies pressed into the twisted metal and puddled plastic embrace of the once alive washing machines, did the area-dwellers sleep; their rent sleep healed.

The morning after the fire, calls to the hospital had found in stable condition not only Short Hair who had suffered the graver injury of second degree burns, but also Mrs. Markham who, though the burns she suffered were minor and confined to her legs, had because of the fragility of her age been considered in some danger. The bleary-eyed gathered around motel lobby payphones had hidden the anxiety that pierced through them on hearing this good news. They voiced pieties: 'What matters is not things. It's people. That's what matters.'

'Amen,' echoed Bernard Mudiamu who spent his Saturdays pastoring the 'New Voice in the Desert Fellowship of Christ Church,' and added his own: 'Praise the Lord from whom all good things come.' When Emma's mother bristled at this he amended his prayer: 'Sister, bow your head and praise him who is merciful.' But neither Bernard Mudiamu nor Emma's mother were relieved of the conviction that somewhere an account remained to be settled. Unspoken, the collective wisdom held: attendant escape from a conflagrant wind, as had just blown through their lives, was surely a price. What price, they wondered, the wholeness of two hundred fifty-two lives spared? What price, they wondered when they woke untouched the morning after and filled their lungs to capacity? What price, they wondered for each of the ensuing five days as, aware of breath and air, they exulted in the rise and fall of the breast? And at night, resting their heads on one another's chests—husbands and wives, mothers, children, siblings, friends and suddenly-sprung lovers—thrilling to the sonority of the pumping heart, wondered in the dark: what price?

Only very young children were immune to this wonder. They occupied motel closets for hide and seek and invited one another to bathtub parties. In the afternoons they slept with their eyes open in front of *Looney Tunes* and woke with bologna sandwiches squashed to their necks. For five days, under Emma's leadership, the littlest children did battle with fires in motel stairs and howled louder when asked to turn their fire engine siren sound down. On the fifth day after the fire, when the story of the bodies in the basement first made the rounds, the children who had played at discovering these bodies many times over, simply blinked in astonishment at the adults joining in their game. And the adults in their discussion were animated, smiling and giggling as the children did when dead bodies made appearance in their play. The adults were relieved. This once in their lives, they found the price paid for escape from further fragmentation cheap—as cheap as the lives of two strangers, perhaps bums who had found their way in to the building basement to sleep away drink.

Emma alone was distraught. Once she understood the bodies were real, she decided they were the bodies of her father and sister who had come back to the building to live as a family again. At times she thought they had remained in the building all along, never leaving it, hiding there and watching over her. Other times she thought they had heard of the fire and come to rescue the family, gotten there before the firefighters, entered the building, and remained trapped there once the doors were sealed.

In the worst moments, she tore at her mother: 'You shouldn't have let them leave. You were mean to Daddy. You never even gave him a glass of water when he asked. You didn't love him. He'd have stayed if you'd loved him. It's your fault.'

Unexpressed was the calculation in her mind of the many sins she had committed: the times she had wished for a father who wasn't a dark cloud suffocating her from the corners he hovered in; the times she had woken from dreams of herself pinned under his legs and thrashed her own legs in twisted sheets to feel them hers again; the times she had muttered when he, home in the middle of the afternoon, roused himself from the couch moments after chuckling at the show on TV and, cursing disapproval at the trash his children watched, turned the set off; the times he had asked her to bring him a glass of water and she had pretended to not hear.

The clean-up of the building took three weeks. Emma no longer led the children in play in the motel's hallways, and absent their leader the children lost their confidence in themselves as a gang. They were sent to school again during the day and come evening they ate using more county-issued vouchers in splintered groups in the parking lots of fast food restaurants. During that time Emma's mother told her that the Coroner had found the bodies were of two men, both of them too old to be that of her father. Months after her mother moved them, at first back into the old apartment and then to another neighborhood, Emma's father called them and confirmed for Emma that he was alive. Her mother said to her then, 'I had to call a lot of people to find him and get him to call here.' Emma only said, 'You just always try to look good.'

'You know what I really liked about your cooking back then?' Emma asks her mother. Her mother's body gives a jump on the narrow bed. Emma knows she is now truly asleep. It's good, she thinks, for her to sleep. And somewhere below the surface ease of that thought lurk less purposeful thoughts: I wish I had some coffee, or even some tea. Yes, tea would be good right now. She says aloud to her mother's back, 'You used to give us tea on school mornings.' Her mother twitches again. Emma walks the length of the bed, rounds the foot and walks to the head. She studies her mother's face. Absent teeth, the mouth is a collapsed tent, but the brow is concentrated in watchful ridges; as if, Emma thinks, she is afraid her hold on life will loosen in sleep. 'Let go,' she whispers to her mother. And as quickly, growing afraid herself, she thinks, Only fifty-eight. She has another twenty years, at least.

Strawberries

KISHORE VALICHA

A man, about forty years old, or forty-five, entered a police station and approached a constable who stood by the door. His voice was low, almost a whisper.

The constable stepped aside, leaned out of the door and spat paan-juice into the verandah. 'Sorry,' he said, 'I couldn't hold it any longer. Yes, so you were saying?' The constable brought his left ear close to the man's mouth and shut his eyes.

The man repeated what he had said. 'I have a complaint.' He appeared timid, unsure of himself. The constable gestured to him to follow.

The constable walked through a dusky corridor lit by a single high powered ceiling lamp. The man followed. An official in heavy khaki who was walking past noticed the man. He stopped briefly. He was elderly, with gray hair and a heavily moustached, plump face. He wore thick glasses. In a Bombay police station, he looked incongruously kind. He narrowed his eyes on account of the glare from the ceiling lamp and asked the constable, 'What is it?'

The constable nodded his head towards the timid man and said, 'Complaint.' The official showed no further interest. He walked on.

In a room at the end of the corridor, a buck-toothed policeman sat staring at a large register placed on a grey metal table in front of him. There was a heavy pen lying on top of the register.

The constable, who had preceded the man, said, 'He has a complaint,' and left.

The buck-toothed policeman did not look up. It was as though he was considering the matter.

'Is it worthwhile?' he asked.

The man did not answer.

'Is it worth the trouble?' he asked again.

The man did not reply.

'Writing a complaint is a tough job, it's like writing an exam. Each time I write a complaint I am reminded of the time I used to write essays at school. I used to sweat with the effort, I had palpitations. My mind ached and my heart turned to ashes.'

The man stood waiting.

The buck-toothed policeman rubbed his eyes and said, 'One of my teachers used to assign an essay once a week; that was her way of meting out punishment, it was torture.' He banged the large register with his fist. 'Torture. Do you understand?'

The impact was so great that it threw the heavy pen, which lay on the register, up into the air. The pen landed on the floor, a little away from the table, and broke into two pieces.

The man bent down, picked up the pieces and handed them to the policeman. The policeman said, 'Now look what you've done.'

The man said, 'I'm sorry.'

'I'll have to requisition a new pen,' the policeman said. 'That will take time, until then I can't write your complaint. Come back tomorrow or the day after, depending on your convenience.'

The man put his hand into his shirt pocket and produced a pen. He held it out to the policeman.

'I can't use your pen,' the buck-toothed policeman pointed out. 'That would be improper.'

He looked up at the man who seemed puzzled.

'I have to record a complaint officially,' he explained, 'using official stationery and official writing implements. That may not be clear to a layman like you, you may think I am only being fussy, but you are wrong. Such details are important, especially when you face a magistrate in court.' This time he brought his open hand down on the complaints register. 'Do you understand?'

The man nodded. It was a slow, uncertain nod.

'If the magistrate questions you in court in the presence of lawyers and higher police officials,' the policeman went on, 'you have to speak clearly and boldly. You have to state that the complaint was recorded in the official complaints book, using an official pen, not the pen of the complainant; using the pen of the complainant or of a private individual or a private pen would amount to misuse of the official complaints register and the complaint would cease to be bona fide. I have no choice but to wait for an official pen for which, as I have said, I will make out a requisition as soon as you leave. Until then your complaint will have to wait.'

The man nodded again. Putting his pen back in his shirt pocket, he turned around and began to walk out. He looked bereaved.

On his way out, he noticed the elderly official who had stopped by him in the corridor with the high-powered ceiling lamp. For a very brief moment, the man paused. The official saw him, and said, 'Can I help you?'

The man murmured something. 'Speak up,' the official said, 'don't be afraid. I am the Inspector, I am in charge of the police station.'

The man tried to raise his voice but faltered.

'Raise your voice a bit, don't be afraid,' the Inspector repeated. He spoke in an encouraging manner; he even smiled.

The man tried. The effort still seemed too great. He failed.

'Come into my room,' the Inspector said.

He led the man through another long passage. Along the floor, stacked against the walls, were damaged tables and chairs. Some of the table tops held old and decaying records of complaints. The pages reeked of old ink, urine and musk. The man inhaled deeply, but discreetly.

Finally the Inspector entered a room. The man followed.

'Sit down,' said the Inspector, pointing to a hard wooden chair. His manner was friendly.

The man kept standing, a little uncertain.

'Here, let me help you,' the Inspector said and, placing his right hand on the man's shoulder, gave him a gentle push. The man lowered himself into the chair.

'This is a terrible place,' said the Inspector sitting down. 'I admit it, and with no hesitation, mind you. I wouldn't mind saying it in public. Let the whole world know, this is a terrible, terrible place.'

He smiled. It was the smile of a man who felt suddenly pleased with his own words. It was, almost, a smug smile.

'You see?' he said to the man. 'I know exactly how you feel.'

The man said nothing.

'Now tell me,' said the Inspector and raised his arms and folded his hands under his chin.

The man hesitated. He tried to find the right words—the right words were crucial to his complaint.

'I've been cheated,' the man said at last.

The Inspector beamed at the man. 'Ah! I'm sorry to hear that,' he said. 'It happens all the time; it's an evil world we live in, and this is a bad, bad city.'

The man nodded. 'Yes,' he said.

'It's tough,' continued the Inspector, 'being good in a hard, bad world. You keep trying, until you see it's a waste of time. Look at the constitution of the world, it's full of rogues and scoundrels,' and, turning to the man, he concluded, 'You see what I mean? It's *kalyug*.'

The man nodded again.

'Today,' said the Inspector, 'is my last day here; I'm retiring tomorrow. I won't come to this place again, ever. I won't have to put on a uniform and sit across this hard table any more. I won't have to pore over these yellow, dusty files full of rotting paper. I won't have to listen to complaints and pass orders and follow up cases and interrogate hardened criminals—lying bastards who crave third-degree. I won't have to appear in court and look at a judge and make false statements. You see what I mean?'

The man smiled, briefly, feeling a little relaxed.

'It's over for me,' went on the Inspector. 'On my last day I want to do something special, something honest and true. I want to help someone on my last day, someone like you, good and meek and humble and perhaps a little servile, a natural prey and target for the vicious. And a great sufferer too, I can tell, a simple man, a poet of the conscience. Do you follow me?'

The man nodded a slow yes.

'Good,' said the Inspector, 'so we understand each other. Tell me who has cheated you.'

'The strawberry woman,' said the man.

The Inspector looked a little puzzled. 'Strawberry?' he said.

'Yes.'

'Strawberry. Isn't that... a somewhat rare fruit?'

The man nodded. Twice.

'In our country,' said the Inspector thoughtfully, 'strawberries grow in cool climates and on hill stations. You get them only for a short while in the right season.'

'Yes,' agreed the man.

'Are you talking of strawberries, then?' asked the Inspector.

'The strawberry woman,' corrected the man. 'The one who sells strawberries at the bus stand.'

The Inspector thought this over. 'What about her?' he asked.

'She cheated me.'

The Inspector looked a bit disappointed. He shook his head and said, 'You say she cheated you?'

'Yes.'

'How did she do that?'

The man took a deep breath. 'I like strawberries,' he explained. 'I can't resist buying them.'

He fell silent. It was as though he felt suddenly oppressed by the weight of the confession he had just made.

'I suppose that is how it is with strawberries,' said the Inspector. 'I can imagine how hard it must be to resist that delectable little fruit.' He sat back. He looked a little smug once again. 'You see,' he said to the man, 'I understand you.'

The man said nothing.

'Go on,' coaxed the Inspector, 'tell me your story. I want to hear it.'

'It happens every strawberry season,' the man began. 'I go out and see the golden orange-scarlet body, and the bit of green leaf on top of each little fruit. I look at the pretty cartons lined with the ripest strawberries, and I can't resist them. I select the carton that seems to hold the best and the largest fruit. I spend hours to do that. I compare one carton with another and then another and so on until I finally decide. It is like buying an exotic picture postcard. You have to go about it with care and thoroughness.'

'Did you buy one?' asked the Inspector.

'Yes. I went to the bus stand and spotted this woman. I had seen her and her strawberries a few times. But I had waited for the larger fruit to arrive, the fruit that comes late in the season. I wanted to take the best home. My mother makes jam with them. She is very old and does not move around very much, but she still makes a fine, rich jam. I help her with it.'

'So you bought a carton?' asked the Inspector.

The man thought for a moment. 'Yes and no,' he said.

'What do you mean?'

'I did buy one,' the man answered. 'It had the largest strawberries I have ever seen. They looked so good, I did not have the heart to let my mother cut them into pieces to make jam. Instead, I put them in a plate and placed them on the dining table. I wanted to watch them glow in the morning as the first sunlight comes sweeping in through the window with the four metal bars. I wanted to see them shine in the light of the electric bulbs at night—we have a small chandelier directly above the dining table. I thought that only after I have feasted my eyes on them for a long enough time would I help my mother cut them into pieces and put them into the pot to make jam. She makes delicious strawberry jam.'

The Inspector leaned forward, with his forearms on the table. 'What is the jam like? It must be special.'

'It's different,' the man explained. 'Not very consistent, for it's made of natural fruit without flavourings and additives. Its texture is creamy and thick and it does not spread evenly. That is what makes it addictive: each time you take a bite of the toast, you taste nippy fruit, the kind that would be a little shrunken, a bit knotty, and hard. But as you chew, it releases a taste that is both very familiar and very strange. It is like being in a specially scented wood... It is the smell of a forest, of wild animals. Exotic animals.'

'I knew the moment I saw you that you are a man of refinement. You are a poet!' the inspector said, and held out his hand over the table.

The man obliged and placed his hand in the Inspector's. The Inspector took it and pressed it for a small moment before returning it.

'So,' said the Inspector, 'you got your strawberries.'

'I did,' said the man, 'and I did not.'

The Inspector considered this statement. He said, 'I understand you bought the strawberries from the woman. Isn't that correct?'

'Yes,' replied the man, 'and I took them home. I helped my mother up in bed and showed them to her. She was also amazed to see such large strawberries. We examined the skin—strawberries have a skin which is uneven, with tiny dot-like lumps, but these ones had skin that was even, smooth and delicately coloured with varying hues of moist orange and scarlet. It was as though each strawberry had been individually hand-painted, and lit from the inside. We handled them with care, tenderly, and placed them on the dining table. We felt we had found a treasure.'

The man paused. He looked at the Inspector to see if he had made his point. The Inspector nodded and smiled.

'It took some time,' continued the man, 'almost a week, for me to realize they were fake.'

The Inspector looked interested. He waited for the man to go on.

'They looked good. But they were not the real thing. Even after a week they remained exactly as they were. They did not ripen further, there wasn't the smallest wrinkle on the skin. The woman had given me something artificial. At first I thought it was all right; they still looked like strawberries and they looked good. I thought we might as well preserve them as works of art. We could derive pleasure by just looking at them, almost the same pleasure as one gets from gazing at striped zebras, at lions with their heavy, ancient manes, at spotted deer with liquid eyes, at green- and red-coloured forest birds, or at genuine strawberries.'

The inspector nodded. 'Yes, that seems practical.'

'But,' said the man, 'they began to crack. One afternoon, I heard strange sounds emanating from them, faint at first. My mother and I put our ears closer to hear the sounds more clearly. It was as though there was life in those strawberries, live things trying to push their way out.'

The Inspector looked thoughtful. 'Eggs?' he asked.

'Yes. Those were eggs, not strawberries. I had been tricked.'

The Inspector said nothing. He waited for the man to continue.

'I suspect the paint on the shells had helped maintain the temperature, and the eggs finally hatched. Little birds, so small that we had to look with care, struggled out. They twittered and trembled violently. Their eyes were shut and their beaks were so tiny and slender that I was afraid they would break. I lifted them as gently as I could and put them in a safe place.'

'Did the birds survive?' asked the Inspector.

'I offered them food,' the man said. 'My mother, though she is frail and rarely leaves her soiled bed without my help, even she found the strength to give them drops of strawberry jam left over from last year. The birds grew a little, and after a few days they stood on their legs and stretched their wings. They gained strength and turned into golden-hued orange and scarlet strawberry birds. They crooned to each other and constantly pruned their feathers with their tiny beaks and made quaint and funny sounds. They were beautiful.'

The Inspector stared at the man.

'We watched them,' the man continued, 'as they waved their little wings in the air and took flight.'

'Strawberry birds?' murmured the Inspector.

'They circled around above our heads. We kept turning round and round trying to keep the birds in focus, marvelling at the precision of their flight, as though they knew the exact circumference of the room and the height of the ceiling. I called out to them and my mother made soft, gurgling sounds, even as our heads reeled from the effort of keeping track of them. I wished them to return to us, to nestle on our shoulders, on our arms and hands, to stay for some more time with us, close to us, to let us watch and savour the extraordinary lightness we witnessed in them.'

The Inspector remained silent. He watched the man's face.

'But, entirely absorbed in their first experience of flight, they were too far away from us to care. They weaved and glided around with such joy and freedom that, as we watched, we felt deprived and impoverished. We felt like destitutes.'

The Inspector said nothing.

'Finally, the birds angled their heads a little and in a split second shifted into a straight path and flew out of the room, through the open window with the four metal bars. Each bird followed the other in precise order into the sky.'

The Inspector leaned back in his chair and looked up at the ceiling. After a while, he turned to the man and studied his face. He took in his sunken eyes, his thick, protruding lips and the coarse salt-and-pepper hair.

'Under normal circumstances,' the Inspector said, 'one needs proof, hard evidence, to punish the guilty.'

'The birds that flew away,' he continued after a pause, 'might perhaps have constituted evidence. The only other evidence is the egg shells, which I don't suppose you have preserved. The shells could have been analyzed and certain facts about the bird species established. One could also work with statements from independent, impartial witnesses, but I presume there are none. Not that their testimony would have formed direct proof, but it might have helped.'

The man looked directly at the Inspector, and kept his gaze on him as the Inspector rubbed his chin and leaned forward.

'But I am not going to insist on proof, because I don't care for it. To me, personally, there's no such thing as proof; proof is only a certain kind of reading of available facts, a statement of articulate, well-spoken power. I am not going to take on the role of a typical police officer. Not today, not on my last day.'

The man heard the Inspector in silence.

'Tell me,' said the Inspector, 'what is it you want?'

The man murmured something. Suddenly, his voice was almost inaudible.

'Should I drag the strawberry woman here?' the Inspector asked.

The man did not reply.

'I can,' the Inspector continued, 'charge her with the crime. I can even make her confess. There are methods, as you know, for extracting a confession; our methods, though a little crude, are good, they save time and help bring about quick admission. Words pour out of the accused in a few short moments of intensity and awakening. We move away as we behold a battered ego declaring guilt; we offer the accused cool water and a cup of hot tea and some refreshment; we feel awed and humbled by the spectacle of what we have achieved.'

The Inspector looked into the man's eyes. 'Is that what you want?' he asked.

The man looked up. 'Something about her...' he said. He did not complete the sentence. 'She cheated me,' he said and stopped. A look appeared on his face and it was soon gone.

'Did she pressurize you?' the Inspector asked patiently. 'Was there something she wanted from you and you refused?'

'She questioned my way of looking at the strawberries,' the man explained. 'Her youthful arrogance, I suspect, led her to do that. She said strawberries were for the passionate, for those with real hunger and an urge for dreams. They were not for the dull and the unadventurous. She kept saying this even as I looked at the strawberries and compared one carton with the other. She said these things with her eyes and her wet painted lips.'

The Inspector leaned sideways in his chair and picked up a glass and a stainless steel jug from a side table to his left. He poured water into the glass, filled it to the rim. He offered it to the man, who declined. The Inspector drank a few mouthfuls.

'It got worse,' the man went on. 'She began preventing me from seeing the strawberries clearly or examining them the way I wanted to.'

'How did she do that?'

'She distracted me. She interjected herself between me and the strawberries. She crept up like a vain and snooty purple shadow playing hide and seek with the strawberries. She opened each box briefly and quickly shut it even before I could quite see the fruit. There was something capricious about that, a little insulting. She then began quoting exorbitant, outrageous prices and she laughed as she did that. She tried to fluster and bewilder me.'

'Do you think,' the Inspector asked, 'all the strawberries were eggs?'

The man thought for a moment before answering. 'She spoke to the strawberries, which was odd,' he said. 'She called them her precious, priceless treasures. She called them endearing names—my little red pearls, she said. Shine, shine, little orbs, she said, shine with heat and passion. She carried on as though I wasn't there.'

'You could have left,' the inspector said. 'You didn't have to listen to her.'

'She hooked me,' the man responded. 'She hooked me by accentuating her sex and by daring me. She hinted at some kind of intimacy between us and cast a spell on me. I tried to resist, I tried to leave, but she used her sensuality to mock me, and because she did that, I was transfixed. I felt weak. She saw that; she saw my attention shift from the strawberries to her body, to her sex, and a secret line of communication opened up between us.'

The Inspector wiped his forehead with the back of his wrist. He listened intently.

'She grew on me,' the man said. 'She seemed suddenly fluid

and expressive, more youthful and base. Gradually she revealed more of her body to me. She did that without being overt; she used simple, suggestive gestures. Even when I turned my gaze to look at the strawberries, she managed to put herself before my eyes. She filled my nostrils with the scent of her body.'

The Inspector asked, 'Did she...?' He left the question unfinished.

'She revealed the contours, the shape and size of her breasts to me,' the man confided. 'It was a casual show, the eroticism was almost unintended. Next, she attracted my attention to her belly and then to the regions below. I could smell her. She moved, a little indecently, to highlight the general roundness of the pelvic region. I felt compelled to look at her and she saw that and she understood. She even spoke of it, in snatches of sentences that she put in her trade talk, in fleeting allusions. She made unctuous, slippery half-statements. She drew unnecessary attention to her full-blown, arrogant figure, to the pure physical energy she had become. She did this in an oblique fashion. It was a signal to me. I understood.'

The man stopped abruptly and looked at the Inspector, as if for encouragement. The Inspector nodded to the man to go on.

'The strawberries were no mere fruit any more. She hadn't observed the rules—this was not a buy-and-sell transaction; it was sorcery. She had used my passion for strawberries to capture something that was beyond what it was all about. I felt awed by her.'

'Did you...?' Once again the Inspector began a question and did not complete it.

'You must understand that I felt appreciation for her magic,' the man continued. 'For a moment it seemed to me that I understood everything, and if that was how it was, that was how it must be. I felt bold and strong. I pointed to a box of strawberries and I said decisively, I'll take these. But she remained where she was and was silent, though she was watching me, and suddenly I wasn't sure and said, No, and pointing to another carton, said, I'll take those. Then I wavered again and said, No, I'll take those—and again, within a moment, I wavered yet again and said, No, not that box, the other one. She noticed the uncertainty, the doubt and she smiled. It was a slow smile, a little contemptuous. It was too wide a smile. I saw her teeth, and her flickering tongue through a small gap in her teeth. She did not look at me after that and did not care to respond as I kept saying, I want that box of strawberries… no, that one… no, no, the other one…'

The Inspector's hand touched the glass half-full with water. He said nothing. He did not drink from the glass.

'Finally she spoke. I understand, she said, I understand you can't make up your mind, and you have no one to make it up for you. And then she giggled and her whole body shook and soon her giggling turned to hard and heavy laughter, uncontrollable laughter that spilled out of her body and bounced all around her like tiny rubber balls. Her eyes began to roll wildly and she began to dance. Her breasts shook and wobbled and her arms swayed in the air. Soon her body lost its balance and swerved first to the left, then to the right, and revealed itself most plainly now, as a house with all its doors and windows ajar would, and finally she fell upon me and I, to keep my balance, grabbed her even as she grabbed me and we clung to each other for quite a while.'

The Inspector sighed loudly. He said nothing.

'Luckily, no one noticed,' the man said. 'There were not many people about; of the three who could be seen waiting at the bus stand one was reading a newspaper and the other two were having an argument, staring into each other's eyes.'

'Did she give you the strawberries?' asked the Inspector.

'I loosened my grip on her. She straightened herself and said, I will choose a box of strawberries for you. She gathered her loose skirt, tucked it between her legs and squatted on the roadside. She ran her fingers over the cartons stacked one top of the other and finally found the one she was looking for. She extricated it carefully without tilting the stack. She uncovered the box and brought it close for my inspection. Look, she said, have you ever seen strawberries more luscious?'

'Were those the eggs?' the Inspector asked.

'I did not look,' replied the man. 'I had no wish to see. I withdrew money from my pocket—I don't know how much—and I paid her. She put the notes inside her blouse, between her breasts, like a vegetable seller or a fisherwoman, though she was clearly neither. She did not count the money. As I got ready to leave, she turned away from me.'

There was a brief pause. The Inspector picked up the glass and drank all the water. He placed the empty glass on the table.

'She cheated me,' the man said, 'she gave me birds' eggs, not strawberries.'

The Inspector nodded.

'I want her punished,' the man said. 'Humiliated.'

'I understand,' the Inspector answered.

'When...?' asked the man.

'Tomorrow,' promised the Inspector, 'tomorrow.' He smiled and picked up the phone on his table to order tea and biscuits.

'Thank you,' the man said and sat back in his chair.

Whorl

VIJAY PARTHASARATHY

We were still innocent, my cousin Vishakha and I, that summer vacation afternoon when we locked ourselves inside the old shed at the bottom of my garden and, in the quiet, rustled out of our clothes for the first time.

We took turns at that, of course. We were playing Doctor— she was going first with me as her patient (because she was the older one by two years, to the day), and she insisted that doctors were always fully clothed. Back then she was a thin girl with thick glasses and funny teeth; when she smiled an incisor jutted out. Take everything off behind this curtain, she instructed, gesturing at an imaginary screen, and hold this towel in front of your thing—I don't want to see your thing.

Her brother, hunched in a corner over a big box of gardening tools, giggled; I glared at him. Vishakha turned her back upon me self-righteously and set up her instruments. I emerged for my examination, shivering slightly in the dampness as she slid a finger down my bony chest, tapping here, rubbing there checking for fractures. She probed my navel, which made me want to piss urgently. Now I have to see your thing, she announced, maintaining a professional air. She pushed my towel away and gripped my erection, first with her right hand, then her left. Does it hurt when I squeeze it?

Vishakha was not academically inclined like I was. We attended the same posh day school in the heart of Bombay, though Vishakha and Gautam lived in the south of the city and I came from suburban Bandra. We didn't often see each other outside of school, except during vacations, but when our names cropped up at family dinners and intimate social gatherings, I was invariably referred to as The Smart One, predestined for a career in engineering because I was good at arithmetic and liked making paper models of airplanes; whereas Vishakha, having made the tennis and swimming teams before turning thirteen, was That Girl.

She didn't care that I knew Papeete was the capital of French Polynesia, or that as a ten-year-old I had accidentally discovered Euler's formula for any convex polyhedron, $F + V = E + 2$, by myself, one morning in the middle of a Moral Science sermon. My cousin wasn't into that sort of thing. The tennis coach saw potential in this girl who had upended the school's second-ranked male player in a practice match; I was more impressed when she told me she had kissed the school's star long distance runner, a boy four years her senior. Perhaps because she was my cousin—and the irony was lost on me then—I was bold with her in school. Typically, during the recess break, if we bumped into each other in one of the loud crowded passageways, I would pull her hair teasingly and she would make a face; if I felt especially courageous, I would put an arm around her shoulder.

It helped that she was an accomplice. Kissing would have somehow compromised our unspoken pact, but always, while playing in her house and hiding from Gautam behind cupboards or curtains in the darkness—me breathing behind her ear, my palms scooping her breasts as she pressed close against me—we persuaded each other to stay concealed for a few moments.

On her fifteenth birthday (and my thirteenth), Vishakha drew me aside and told me she had decided to become a movie star, and made me swear that I would keep it a secret, although later I discovered I wasn't the only person she had confided in. And she said it like that, too—'I've decided'—at once thrillingly wilful and complacent.

We were hosting a combined birthday party that evening in her seventeenth floor flat for our school friends, both hers and mine, and it annoyed me to see how popular she was. She had more male friends than I did. She was easy on the eyes, no question, tall and loose-limbed, with a wingspan that stretched the limits of graceful. Her nose had lost its fleshiness and her dark complexion emphasised the high cheekbones and angular jaw; braces had fixed her teeth and she had switched to contact lenses. To my adolescent mind she was shapely. In the make-up she had lately taken to wearing she looked older and unapproachable.

Her father—my mother's brother—drew a line at the fifth ear piercing. He said she was succumbing to a fad, but her mother (who wore a different pair of emerald ear-studs for each day of the week) said she looked beautiful and his objection was, for once, overruled. My uncle ran the flourishing family business in textiles, but like many whose roots are steeped in old money, he was a conservative and deeply mistrustful of what he perceived as Vishakha's increasingly mutinous manner. Yet he was a rebel in his own time: growing up in Madras in the 1960s, he would play LPs of the Beatles in place of Suprabhatam every morning.

My uncle thought I was a sobering influence on his son. In truth, Gautam was growing to be excruciatingly awkward; there was nothing I could have done for him. He was quietly plump, effete and insecure. We took swimming lessons together at the Gymkhana Club pool one summer—I to gain height, he to lose weight—and he persistently refused to strip to his trunks until our exasperated instructor made an exception and allowed him into the pool with his shirt on. Even later, when he had grasped the fundamentals, he preferred to sit poolside in the sun and dip his feet in the cold water, and would merely shake his head if I splashed some in his face. He was closer to Vishakha and she in turn adored him. He escaped much of the physical ragging that one faced in the playground simply because so many boys harboured a crush on his sister.

Vishakha attended anthropology lectures at St. Xaviers' College, participated in theatre productions, and dreamed of attending The Juilliard School in New York. She was discovered one afternoon, as it goes, browsing at a designer boutique that had opened near Jaslok Hospital on Peddar Road. Its Punjabi owner, a minor fashion designer, asked her to model his line for a modest fee; elated, Vishakha signed the contract a week after turning eighteen without having consulted her parents. Even so, she wasn't naïve and took no notice of the minor fashion designer's pleas for a seduction. When the pictures arrived, she saw that her face had been cut out; the patron had failed to communicate that he specifically admired the way miniskirts fell around her legs. The relief at not having to reveal all to her parents outweighed any disappointment and she was able to move on and open a portfolio. A second offer came through, this time to promote earrings; then another; and shortly afterward, someone in a position of influence noticed her face.

She then confessed to her mother, who once again proved remarkably supportive, if critical of her daughter's deceit.

I chose jurisprudence instead. I moved to cool unpolluted North Bangalore and into the boys' hostel on campus at the National Law School. In my first year I shared with two others, a room significantly smaller than the kitchen, back home. For privacy we had to make do with curtains. The maids cleaned out the common dormitory toilets every afternoon; if I was unable to wake up early enough, I would find nougats of shit floating in our squat-hole. Before the first month was up, our books were starting to compete for space with Coke cans and ashtrays.

By the end of the semester, we were competing with seniors for female attention. I liked my new independence, and repeatedly put off visits home. Long hair didn't suit my face, so I cultivated a goatee. As my focus on academics blurred, my lifestyle unwound. I made drinking buddies. In my second year, one of them crashed blindly into a road divider at eighty miles an hour, and the rest of us swore to keep off weed and cigarettes and alcohol; three months passed before we felt able to party again. I fumbled through sexual encounters in that promiscuous environment. Emotional connections were severed as frequently as they formed.

I attempted to restore communication with some schoolmates. Gautam, one of them told me, had joined an Engineering college in Nagpur. His father must have been pleased. I wrote Vishakha an email but received no response. Her pictures were on the Web by then, and I saw her fleetingly on television; it was during a phone conversation with my mother that I learned she had moved out, after college, against her parents' wishes. I took her number, but somehow never called.

Dhadkan, her debut feature length film, opened in my fourth year—it was unsettling to have a life-sized image outstare me. This plush Bollywood project introduced my cousin to lascivious audiences, albeit as 'Maneka' (the name Vishakha did summon the image of a vamp). The thing was a disaster; naturally, I did not reveal the familial association to anyone. But at least I got to see Vishakha.

Her second film, however, proved popular in the metros and was aggressively promoted by the media as a breakthrough for Bollywood cinema. Vishakha, credited this time under her given name, played the lead role of an earnest film journalist. The awards, when they came, were accompanied by high praise: one chairman of the jury, a leading feminist critic, pronounced her the Thinking Woman's Actor.

I didn't think much of the movie. (It made reflexive and inter-textual jokes—concepts one wasn't likely to encounter in a Bollywood film—but was loud and self-indulgent, too, like a bad Salman Rushdie novel, only not nearly as clever.) Vishakha sought my opinion eagerly when I finally called her, so I said that I'd loved it. I was back in Bombay, having just been accepted at Oxford for a Masters, and making preparations to leave. We couldn't meet; she was in Jaipur for a protracted shoot. Our conversation was abrupt and lasted five minutes until she was called away.

I did see Gautam once, at his parents' flat, when I paid them a courtesy call. My uncle patted my shoulder and facetiously suggested that the time had come for him to retire and pass me the reins. At lunch, his wife berated me for not having visited them in five years, and good-naturedly accused me of putting on intellectual airs. Gautam sat stoically through the conversation. His face was rounder, paler and scraggly; perhaps the fuzz reassured him of his sex. I slapped his back and teased him about his celebrity status-by-association; he smiled sheepishly and scratched his cheek.

Hardly searing, as final memories go.

Gautam died before he turned twenty-one, the victim of a misadventure while on vacation with classmates in Madgaon. His high spirited friends had gathered together and pulled him into the sea with his clothes on since he refused to join them without; it was close to ten in the night when they realised he was missing.

Gautam had a lopsided smile on his face, my mother told me in the morning, maybe he hadn't suffered much. He likes being dead, I wanted to reply. I was a week into my legal apprenticeship with Bristows in London, and settling in my tiny rented Kensal Green flat when it happened. It could have been the distance but I didn't feel much after the initial surge of shock, except guilt for not wanting to see the body, which I assuaged by reasoning that I could not have made it in time.

I flew to Bombay for the eleventh day rituals and arrived directly on Altamount Road, wearing stubble and a coat jacket over my most restrained pair of jeans, to take my place alongside my parents, old friends and elapsed relatives, all clad in white kurta-pajamas and shifting restlessly on the floor-mat. My aunt barely comprehended my presence. My uncle smiled weakly when I settled behind him and muttered my condolences. He had a nick under his left ear, from shaving.

Vishakha's entry into the room caused a slight commotion and interrupted the mourning. Some respectfully tried to make way, others tried to snatch a peek. She was in a sombre churidar kurta and looked haggard; she had pouches under her eyes and her mouth drooped. She scanned the room and noticing me, pursed her lips in greeting and squeezed in adjacent.

Vishakha called a few months after the cremation, as winter

was setting in. She was in London for a few days, she said. We met on a weeknight for dinner at my favourite Italian place, near Blackfriars Bridge. I arrived in work clothes and found her sitting on the kerb, surrounded by a group of Indian graduate students on a night out. Several held out digital cameras and asked me to take a picture of them together with my cousin. That took time. She was wrapped not in a long coat but a cream pashmina shawl, which she politely declined to take off.

Once we were inside, she ordered for a bowl of rice and pea soup and nothing else. The restaurant was softly lit and the tables, covered with blue-and-white checked cloth that reached the floor, were closely spaced. Casually she slipped off the shawl to reveal a wool-blend dress that cut deep into her cleavage— madness in this weather, but chic. My reaction gratified her. She looked well but for the fact her cheeks appeared to have sunken slightly. We spoke quietly of Bombay. She reminisced fondly of her old set from college; she was in touch with a few. I asked if she was happy.

'Nobody,' she said with a laugh, 'is ever satisfied with what they have become.'

With arms folded and resting on the table, she watched me pick at the fusilli and potatoes on the plate and blow on my fork. Our knees touched under the table but we didn't withdraw them.

We skipped dessert and took a walk along the Victoria Embankment. It was getting cold and she smiled when I put my arm around her. She hummed a fragment of a tune that had played in the restaurant, an old song that I liked, over and over again. When the bells across the city tolled eleven I asked if she preferred taking a cab to my place. She shook her head and said she wanted to take the underground: at Waterloo we made the last tube to Harrow & Wealdstone.

The living room would seem brighter with a painting or two, she said later, leaning against the kitchen counter, as I fixed us stiff vodkas; it's not big but you could try and make it feel a little more like home. She sank in the couch, holding her glass by the base in an affected style like it contained wine—she sipped loudly too. I turned off the lights—That's better, I said, we don't need paintings now.

Under my weight the couch sank deep. I listened to her breathing grow progressively shallower, in shorter gasps; I reached out and ran my finger down the bridge of her nose. The radio droned in the background, barely audible, like a distant helicopter. I gulped down my drink in one shot and shut my eyes tight. That afternoon, I said, smiling, grimacing, with my eyes still closed—when we were kids, in my shed? I was so angry with Gautam after he told your father; it was embarrassing.

She snuggled up to me and, resting her head against my chest, gave me a light hug; I hugged her back, unyielding, my eyes stinging from the vodka, and although after that I was unable to say much, I knew we were grateful for the company.

Kailla

NEEL KAMAL PURI

When Kailla disappeared on the first day of November in 1984, it was generally expected that he would be back. He performed this trick often. He was the rabbit in the hat. He was also the magician. A *chhoo-mantar* mumbled over the hat, and it was empty. It could be held up to the audience, twisted, turned upside down, dusted out, but no Kailla. Ten days later, or twenty, he would reappear, roll up his sleeves and resume his vigil over the flowers and the fruits.

But when he disappeared that November, it was for the last time. After that, old Jassi's house slipped off the wheel of time, too tired to keep pace. A field of matted weeds threatened to swamp it. A forest of brooding trees threatened to choke it. All the children of the neighbourhood knew there was no one to stop them now if they went in to raid the trees for fruit, but few of them did. It wasn't as much fun as it used to be.

There was a time when the soothing music of a spoon in Jassi's afternoon cup of tea was almost always interrupted by Kailla's rant. '*Kaille da kalesh*', she called it. It had to have a name, because it had become institutionalized. It happened every day. '*Oye!* Just you wait—I'm coming!' he would shout to the children who crept in from the neighbouring settlement. They came not only to steal the fruits, but also for the entertainment of the chase. 'You just wait, you langurs, wait till I catch you!' Kailla would rush out of the outhouse and half run half hobble after them, the bottoms of his striped pyjamas flapping. The clumsy swirls of his turban usually came undone the minute he moved. The langurs led him round the compound till he ran out of expletives and then sped away, shouting, '*Chacha*, we'll see you tomorrow. Can't wait just now, we're in a hurry.'

Once, Jassi had tried to reason with him. 'Why don't you let the children eat some of the fruit? At least you'll have less work clearing the grounds of rotten stuff.'

Kailla had been indignant. 'Let them plunder the *trees*, Bibi! Should I just stand and *watch*? It takes years upon years to grow roots, Bibi. You have no idea what hard work it is to make a tree grow, then make it flower and fruit. I've grown old in this same soil tending to these trees!' He hadn't spoken to Jassi for days after that, and she had never again interfered.

Now when the stray child came in, she watched from the window and half expected to see Kailla in pursuit. But there was no shout, nor the urgent scuffling of swift young feet. Jassi wondered why she was still here and not with her sons in Canada. She stayed, perhaps, for the same reasons that Kailla did. Though she never knew what they were.

*

Kailla had moved into the outhouse with his parents shortly after Jassi's husband was born. He was Shafi then. His father worked in a hosiery and did odd jobs for the household, while his mother cooked and cleaned in the *kothi*. They were devout Muslims and went to offer namaz every Friday, *jumme ke jumme*, at the Jama Masjid in Field Ganj.

Religion then, like now, was a whole meal—a bit of god, a

bit of socializing and a bit of politics. But for four- and five-year-olds like Shafi, god meant little, and politics nothing at all. Yet there *was* a charge in the air that even they could feel, not all the time, but at sudden moments when adult faces went red and the voices acquired the high-pitched twang of a taut wire. Shafi would look up from play at such moments and instinctively run to his mother and hold her hand.

He had held her hand all the while that his mother and ten-twelve khalas, his mother's friends (those in burqas he recognized by their *chappals*), had walked through the city in a large crowd shouting slogans. It was the 20th day of December in the year 1921, and a rumour had gone round. It made all the adults around Shafi go red in the face. Maulana Habib-ur-Rehman Ludhianvi, great-grandson of Ludhiana's own Shah Abdul Qadir who had bravely led the mutineers on to Delhi in 1857, had been put to death inside the city jail. 'Over sixty years and a whole generation later, the firangis are still exacting revenge!' Shafi's father had said in a voice so high-pitched, sounding so much like his wife, that his son had momentarily lost all fear of him.

Like Shafi's father, at least half of Ludhiana was already in protest mode before the rumour began. Mahatma Gandhi had addressed a huge gathering at Daresi Ground earlier that year, exhorting people to adopt non-cooperation. There were a series of events in the months that followed, and soon people had fine-tuned satyagrah into strategic action to suit their local resources. So in the last month of the year 1921, first a hundred blind students from the madrassa were raising slogans in front of the clock tower. Then women—Muslim, Hindu and Sikh—and a few children, Shafi among them, were marching in the streets to protest the killing of Maulana Ludhianvi. The British could not touch either of these processions. The police had to bring the Maulana out of jail and show him to the public before they were satisfied. But a handcuffed Maulana was an even greater incitement to join Gandhi's satyagrah. And so it was that the Muslims of Ludhiana aligned with the Mahatma, and stayed with the Congress even when there were demands elsewhere for a separate Muslim nation.

But in '47, most of them left the city for Pakistan. Shafi was among the few who stayed.

He was a carefree young man in the early forties, uncomplicated and easy to please. He worked in the old hosiery that was now a factory, weaving fabric on the same loom as his father. He would walk to work—always ten minutes after his father left—whistling tunes he'd made up, and smiling to himself as though he was holding down the only secret worth the keeping in all of Ludhiana. As part of his duties for the day, he was also required to escort Jassi's sister-in-law to college and back. He would carry her books and follow her faithfully, half in love with the idea of being in love, imagining for himself the role of a persecuted lover who had dared to fall in love with the *malik*'s daughter. Or he would be slaying demons ten times his size as he followed his charge. A swipe from the thickest book in his arms (Vincent A. Smith's *Oxford History of India*) would catch many a *rakshas* square in the middle of the forehead, and the horned beast would collapse in a heap blubbering apologies for daring to covet the fairest girl in Punjab.

Sometimes, he was the doomed Ranjha, and she the beautiful Heer whom the world would deny him. But he never let his mind wander too far into the messy business of misunderstandings and death. He was too full of life to be the hero of a tragic love legend, even in his dreams.

When Jassi's sister-in-law was married and left the house, Shafi mooned around for a bit because that was a requirement of the role he had assigned to himself. In the kothi they thought he was missing her just the way a brother should and thought of comforting him. But by then he had assumed the role of a jilted lover and the agony of separation had turned into indignation at being thrown over. They were confused to see him walk around looking like thunder, but this lasted exactly eighteen days.

So it was not really for love that Shafi stayed on after the great division. It was for the drama in his head. For the demons that climbed out of it and walked up Ferozpur Road to Bharat Nagar Chowk and onto Mall Road, half way to the college, where he struck them down.

Or perhaps it was for the phantom gathering that he addressed at the Daresi Ground while on his way to the Ludhiana Fort, where the British had set up a textile-weaving unit, a massive boiler with 'John Thompsons, Wolverhampton 1924' printed on it in bold letters. Cutting across the vast Daresi Ground, whistling to himself, he would suddenly stop in his tracks. The temptation was too strong. He always succumbed. The blink of an eye raised a rostrum, and he would be standing next to Gandhi and Nehru.

'Satyagrah and khaddar! Wear only khaddar—none of this foreign-made mill cloth—and we'll have swaraj in eight months!' He stretched out his arms to the surging crowds in appeal. He raised a finger to the sky to make a point. He put fire in the hearts of young and old. 'Since 1919 Punjab has suffered like no other part of Hindustan. It was in Punjab that Hindustan was made to crawl on its belly, it was in Punjab that our leaders were beaten and humiliated and killed! But Punjab has responded poorly to the call of the nation. Not many college students have given up college and not many titled persons have given up their titles. Let us pledge today that with khaddar and ahimsa Punjab will lead Hindustan to swaraj. *Puran* swaraj!'

Shafi awoke many mornings half expecting to hear the city talking of the rising star who rivalled Gandhi and Nehru.

It was for this and perhaps a dozen other reasons that Shafi did not join his parents and extended family when they decided to cross the new border. He was in his late twenties then, though his mind, busy as Ludhiana's bazaars on winter afternoons, was still sixteen. In any case, he had not thought that the choice was so final, that the divide was so absolute that he would never see them again. News floated back some weeks later that his entire family had been massacred in one of the caravans wending its way to Pakistan, except for an uncle and his young son.

Shafi himself had to move out of the outhouse and hide in the main kothi till the killing of Muslims abated. It was difficult to daydream in the narrow store attached to the kitchen, among the sacks of wheat and stacks of *gur*, so he crept out sometimes, climbed a fruit tree in the compound and stayed there for hours. The household accepted his withdrawal with quiet patience, except Jassi's mother-in-law, who berated him for leaving his hideout, till his sullen silence drove her to tears and she reminded him of all the years she'd fed him and clothed him like her own sons and was this any way of repaying her for her kindness, seeking out death in her own house and making her a sinner in the durbar of the *Sachepadshah*?

It was months before things went back to normal in the city

and Shafi could leave the house. Though he wasn't quite his old self yet, and walked only to Jama Masjid. The masjid was now a gurudwara. He made his peace with the change, and instead of offering namaaz, bowed to the Granth Sahib and listened to shabad kirtan. He tried very hard to grow a beard—shaving twice a day, rubbing camel piss and onion juice into his cheeks—and failed, so he wrapped a cloth round his head and announced that he would henceforth be known as Karnail Singh.

Shortly after he assumed the new name, he disappeared for six days. When he returned, he had a blue turban, a kada on his right wrist and a kirpan by his side, though still no beard. He had travelled to Anandpur Sahib, he said, and converted. He would disappear about once every year after that, for periods ranging from a day to some months, and offer no explanation, but each time he returned as a Sikh. When Jama Masjid was reconverted into a mosque in 1956, at the insistence of Pandit Nehru, Shafi continued to be Karnail Singh.

And from there to Kailla was easy.

By the time Jassi came into the house after her marriage, Kailla had recovered all of his imagination. Her children, two sons and a daughter, grew up on elaborate stories of the kind that only Kailla could tell.

'I can make people disappear. I can turn a man into a *jhaadu*,' he would tell them. 'That is what I do when big people misbehave.'

The children were sceptical. 'How can you do that? You are not a magician.'

'I am. Remember the time I went away last year for four months? I lived with a *Bangali jaadugar* and learnt magic from him.'

'Then do some magic for us.'

'No, no. It is not a game, it can be dangerous. I perform magic only when there is no other option.'

The children would challenge him: 'You're saying this only because you don't know any *jaadu-shaadu*. You can't change anyone into a jhaadu.'

'Why would I lie to you? Come, I'll show you.' And he would lead them to the kitchen. 'Do you see all those big *kundi-sottas* lined up against the wall?' he would ask, pointing to the black stone mortars and pestles. 'They were all men once. I turned them to stone because they were wicked. You see this one? It's smooth at the top. Feel it. This used to be a bald man.'

The pestle was worn silky smooth, and the children, more used to seeing turbaned heads, felt it and marvelled at it. 'What did he do to become a sotta in our kitchen?'

'Actually, he was a reincarnation of the Raja of Sunet. You remember the one I told you about?'

'The one who lived on that mound outside Ludhiana and ate people and burped loudly?'

'Yes. I warned him, but he wouldn't stop. He began roasting children and eating them, too. So I had to turn him into a kundi-sotta. Everyone is safe now.'

That was Kailla's justice.

Unlike his uncle's. The old man came on a visit from Lahore many years after '47 and told Kailla how he had settled scores soon after he reached the other side. He had joined a group of Muslim brothers by the railway tracks near Lahore. Each man, he said, had pulled out three *kafirs* and cut them to pieces. Kailla had listened to him in silence in the outhouse, then made him tea.

'Have you never wanted to leave?' his uncle had asked. 'You can stay with us, you can find something to do. We belong there.' And Kailla had shaken his head. 'Is this your home? You think these are your people?' the old man had said roughly, and Kailla had shrugged. 'Should I turn him into a sotta?' he had thought.

Meanwhile, Ludhiana was changing. In the bazaar, shopkeepers were slowly hammering down the thick walls of the Ludhiana Fort to increase the size of their shops. They had to wet the walls and keep them soaked to soften them for slaughter. They would not give way otherwise. These were no ordinary walls. They had been made from the bricks baked in pre-Christian era Sunet. Old timers complained about the changes, about the whittling away of the past, but not Kailla. This was still his city, his space to daydream and make up stories.

In the kothi, Jassi's parents-in-law died within a year of each other. The children grew up and went away to other lands, to Canada and America. When Jassi's husband was paralyzed after a stroke, Kailla gave up his job at the textile mill and for four years he bathed and changed his friend and master, massaged his legs and arms with warm oil, and carried him to the toilet and the open verandah every morning and evening. Kailla also entertained him, pulling on Jassi's cast off petticoat and a matching *kameez* to perform a *mujra*. Occasionally, he grumbled about his lot in life, though more out of a recent habit he had acquired rather than any real rancour—he thought somebody should have found him a girl to marry, and that it was still not too late if they only tried. But he did not disappear during this period.

Kailla did not return to work at the textile unit after Jassi's husband died. She depended on him for most outdoor work, and he was too old-fashioned to leave a woman to fend for herself. Of course, the mill had also changed character, though that didn't bother Kailla, he would have adapted to this change as well. When he started work all those years ago, the weavers usually broke for namaaz five times a day. After Partition, the unit was starved for weavers and Kailla became a master craftsman at the knitting machine. Of late, however, there had been a new influx. Workers from Bihar and UP were coming in by the trainloads to man the power looms and the lathes. They stayed in their own colonies, where the cloth shops sold nylon saris, the *mithai* shops sold *gujiya*, and the general merchant sold Chhokra Sabun and Sri Gange Tel. This was the Hindi heartland in Punjab.

Kailla became a frequent visitor here, because a couple of his old work-mates had shifted to these colonies. He would walk around in the narrow lanes, while away some time sitting at a dhaba-cum-mithai-shop, and periodically fall in love with one or the other woman in the locality, fascinated by the silver rings they wore on their toes. He took to speaking a mix of Punjabi and Hindi, and added Chhat Puja to his list of festivals to be celebrated. He kept his turban, though, and his formal name, Karnail Singh, because it amused the mill workers' wives.

Around this time, Kailla disappeared again and never came back. Jassi remembered well; it was the morning after Indira Gandhi was shot down by her Sikh bodyguards. Some months later, she heard from a boy who came to steal fruit that his father had seen Kailla boarding a train to Delhi with two men from the mill. They were going to attend the Prime Minister's funeral, he had said. For many nights, Jassi saw Kailla in her dreams, burning to molten white inside a circle of howling men.

The Lipstick

UMA GIRISH

She was dusting the dresser when she saw the lipstick. The case was fashionably contoured in turquoise blue with narrow gold linings on the rim. *This is a new one.* What colour could it be? Her mind leapt excitedly at the possibilities. Gold and peach, the colours of dawn; or the luscious red of a watermelon? Maybe it was cocoa brown like the creamy swirls of chocolate she'd seen in the ad on the community television set. Perhaps it was the russet of henna that stained a bride's palms?

Amudha picked up the case gently, ran a finger along its smooth contours, and felt a quick, surreptitious thrill shoot across her eleven-year-old arm. *Open me, it tempted.* No harm in taking a quick peek. She only wanted to discover which of her guesses was right. *Go on*, a deliciously wicked voice inside her head prodded.

'Amudha…' Akka's voice was a neat knife through the girl's soft, sensual dream. Quick as a flash, Amudha replaced the lipstick case and started to drag the duster across the dresser.

'Still not finished?!!'

'Just two minutes, Akka.'

'Hurry up, girl. You can't stand there dusting all day.'

Amudha put her fantasies on hold and moved her hand across the wooden surface with new vigour.

*

Selvi clutched the banister, wincing with every step she climbed. Her knees ached. She dragged her feet up the third and final flight of stairs to 3C. Amudha had finished her chores and left early today. Selvi could see her daughter's young fingers flying with an energetic rhythm as the she transformed a heap of vegetables into perfect circles and cubes, whisked the duster like a magic wand, and sprinkled fresh water in the courtyard to coax the coarse, sweet smell of wet earth. The same fingers grew heavy and weary when they were required to turn the pages of a school reader. The red welts that Selvi regularly inflicted on Amudha's palms did little to improve her attitude to education. If anything, they strengthened her resolve to play truant.

'If you send me there one more day, I'll run away from home,' she'd threatened, eyebrows knit in a serious frown.

'You want to wash vessels and bathrooms all your life? Like me?' Selvi's eyes flashed fire.

In response, Amudha simply wound her index finger around the mango-hued ribbon braided into her dark hair.

Her damp hair shining, and smelling of soap nut powder, she had waited the next morning, dressed in her best skirt and blouse, as Selvi piled a mountain of scoured vessels near the wood stove. Seeing that the girl was not in uniform, Selvi grabbed a broom and hobbled after her waving it menacingly, the veins of its coconut leaves shivering with unuttered threats. Amudha dodged laughing, and followed her to 3C. Soon it came to be an unspoken arrangement. And as time went by, even Selvi saw the benefit—her legs needed fewer massages and turmeric poultices. It seemed like the right time to stop complaining about her daughter's forsaken education.

'What Amudha, new skirt?' Mrs. Ramalingam smiled,

55

uncoiling the white cotton towel her wet hair was wrapped in. The girl swirled, a riot of peacock blue swishing about her ankles. At Mrs. Kamakshi's house next-door there was always a mound of rice soaked in buttermilk and a sliver of lime pickle ready and waiting for her every morning. The lime was so tangy, just a nibble made her eyes squint and her mouth pucker as she bit into it.

'We must find a handsome prince for you, girl. Look at your earrings dancing against your cheek!' said Mrs. Ambika, the second-floor tenant, as she carefully picked and tossed stray stones from a heap of rice grains.

The young girl flashed between apartments and chores, her colourful skirts whirling about her. She didn't consider them chores—what she did brightened homes and brought fresh sparkle to people's lives. As she flicked the broom across the mosaic tiles, fragments of the latest Kollywood number spilled from her lips and she swayed in time to it. When she sprayed water on the front courtyard, her fingers dancing in a sunlit silvery arc, her glass bangles tinkled merrily and made her giggle with the unexpectedness of the moment.

Like the beautiful lotus flower that blossomed in scum, Amudha brought brightness to her surroundings and an otherwise sordid existence. She often forgot herself when in the company of the broken mirror at home. Hours were spent preening into it, her face twisted into mobile expressions of utter delight. While she liked most of what she saw, the one thing that irked her was the colour of her skin—roasted cumin. The *Fair & Lovely* commercials on television made her heart twist with envy. Models, brown as toffee, magically transformed into fair-skinned beauties at the end of thirty seconds. *If only I could afford such a luxury. Someday I will be able to*, she vowed. Her reflection smiled back and reflected a pair of impish eyes that brimmed with life. She smeared her indexfinger with kohl and lined her lower eyelids, and dotted the centre of her forehead with a fluorescent pink *bindi*. It was the perfect match for her pink-and white ankle-length skirt and she was pleased with the effect. The next fifteen minutes were spent weaving her oil-stained fingers in and out of her waist-length strands, the warm smell of coconut oil seasoned with hibiscus flowers rising around her. Then she parted the midnight cloud into equal halves, twisted each into a snake-like braid, and threaded them with pink ribbons. If she was lucky enough to find Raji the flower seller in a benevolent mood, she would get a string of fragrant white jasmine to tuck into her hair.

Amudha's weekly forays to the bazaar were like trips to *Alladin's* cave. She gazed longingly as the sellers spread their wares on the pavement. Bangles in rainbow shades gleamed by the light of the moon; heaps of hair clips shaped like birds and flowers lay in colourful arrays; silver-plated trinkets for toes, ears, and ankles begged to be bought; and, hair bands shone with the magic of the glitter powder strewn on them. Amudha lifted her head and took a deep breath of the smell she loved; warm, roasted peanuts swaying to the tinny tinkle of a ladle that pushed them from side to side. She felt the sweat soak into her armpits as she melded with the jostling crowds. Running up to the cloth merchant she let her fingers caress slinky soft velvet, the material that dressed her in her dreams. Shouting vendors, arguing customers, the hiss of the Petromax lantern as it pooled, hot and golden, on the displayed wares, fresh blobs of cow dung in the middle of the street, toffee wrappers that followed the Pied

Piper-like breeze, cranky toddlers wailing at the loud noise, the press of bodies, people pushing ahead eager to get to the source of temptation for the best bargains—it was a multi-coloured dream Amudha lived week after week, one that never diminished in enchantment.

'Amma, I want those purple hair clips...' Amudha would begin.

'You think money grows on trees? As it is, your father, that good-for-nothing drunk, doesn't give me one paisa. Purple clips! Huh!'

'Amma... please... please... Amma... they look so pretty... they'll match my purple skirt and blouse... please Amma...'

By the end of the evening, Selvi, unable to bear the ceaseless whining, would forfeit her hard-earned money to fund Amudha's fancies.

*

Amudha couldn't wait to get to the dresser each morning. Dusting that piece of furniture was her ticket to fantasyland. She would stand and stare, mesmerized by the array of bottles and jars of lotions that sat in obedient rows. There was the thick, milky-white lotion Akka slathered on her face, neck and arms before she stepped out into the sun; the small oval bottle that contained a gold-coloured liquid which Akka sprayed all over her body, something that made her smell of delicious wild flowers and scented meadows; the talcum powder, a soft, white, sweet-smelling shower, pale pink floral tendrils creeping around its apple-green container; then there were tiny bottles that held opaque liquids, and tubes out of which creams squiggled in pastel shades.

And there was the new lipstick. The turquoise blue case sat up, tall and proud, the lipstick inside waiting to stain a pair of luscious lips.

To Amudha, the rest of the bedroom was a blind spot. She hardly noticed the richly embroidered maroon drapes, the carved teakwood bed, the side-tables that held knick-knacks; and, the throw rugs that burnt a fiery shade of sienna on the mosaic floor. The dresser consumed her fascination and blurred the edges of her vision. Very often, she would be in the living room sweeping stale crumbs into a dustpan when an alien scent of unnamed flowers floated in on the breeze and assaulted her nostrils. *Akka in the middle of her beauty regimen.* Quickly pushing the broom and dustpan to a corner she would slink behind the heavy drapes and watch wide-eyed as Akka uncorked the magic that lived and breathed in those jars. But one morning Akka had caught her out.

'Hey, girl! What are you staring at, huh? Run along. Go and do your work,' she shooed her.

But the image of that lipstick had been burned into Amudha's head. It tinted her ordinary dreams, the full pink of its smooth, shiny texture coating stretched lips until they shone like dawn rosebuds. To have a lipstick of her own! The desire filled every inch of space in her body with a furious yearning. When the second lipstick appeared on the dresser, the urge to discover its shade was like a constant itch, one that refused to go away.

Amudha gently flicked traces of dust off the bottles and jars and lined them up like soldiers on parade, their fashionable labels synchronized in colourful display. She polished the mirror above the dresser until her reflection shone back at her. Then she stood, shoulders thrown back, and made a moue, pursing her bow-shaped lips, hands on hips, and fluttered her eyelashes at the mirror—like the glamorous heroines in the movies. *If only she could colour those lips*!

From the day temptation caught her in its vice-like grip Amudha's mind worked overtime and charted a course of action. The object of her dreams, a lipstick the colour of Selvi's pan-stained mouth, hovered tempting, teasing on the horizon. *She had to have it*. She packed extra hours into her already crowded day, her hands and feet flying with new purpose. She cleaned out Mrs. Swamy's cobweb-ridden loft; washed Mr. Dorai's white Maruti thrice a week; helped Raji string rose garlands for weddings and funerals; cleared out Sami's garage of its chaotic assortment of pipe lengths, rusty tools and broken buckets. Every time she earned a few rupees or coins, she secreted it away carefully in an old Nescafe jar she'd rescued from Mrs. Dorai's garbage bin. Hugging her secret around her like a warm blanket she stretched out on the tattered coir mat bathed in moonlight and dreamed wonderful dreams about coloured lips.

*

And then one day she almost gave it away.

It was a muggy afternoon, the air wet and heavy. Amudha skipped home, a song on her lips, after a morning spent cleaning fans in the corner house. As she pushed open the door to the thatched shanty she heard muffled sniffles. The place was filled with the smell of fresh grief.

'Amma... what happened? Why are you crying?' The girl rushed to Selvi and draped a comforting arm about her.

'It is my fate. I must have been a terrible sinner in my

previous birth. Or why else would I suffer like this today?' Selvi slapped her forehead.

'But what happened? Tell me Amma. Please.'

'What can I say? Your sister-in-law delivered her second stillborn this morning. I told Vasantha Amma about it and she gave me an advance to go to the village. But your father, that... that... son-of-a...' and Selvi's face disappeared into her sari *pallu* again.

'What did he do?'

'I was... I was... counting... the money and he came from behind... grabbed it... and ran out,' Selvi hiccupped the words.

'Now I can't go and see my son and daughter-in-law... be with them at this time...'

Amudha fell silent.

The steadily growing sum in her secret tin flashed through her mind and she felt its satisfying metallic heaviness. She thought of all the movies she'd missed, all the hopscotch games she'd given up to get an extra hour's work done somewhere for some money, tumbling into an exhausted sleep at the end of a hard day... the images unfurled in her head, the many hours of labour with which she'd filled the Nescafe tin.

Amma needed money now. To offer it to her would be the right thing to do. But that would mean putting her dream on hold, refueling it, starting all over again. She saw the red lipstick sprout wings and fly further away, out of reach.

The baby was dead and gone. There were enough relatives in the village to console her brother and sister-in-law, to hold their hands through this passing crisis. In any case Amma must have planned to go only for a day or two. How did it matter? She would say nothing. But why did the space inside her chest feel like a rock? How was she any different from her father if she denied her mother in her hour of need? Wasn't she just as selfish?

Her lips tasted the lipstick, as its rich moisturizer creamed colour over them.

None of this was her fault. *Why did that baby have to die now?* This was her money, money she had rightfully earned by clocking extra hours. She hadn't cheated anyone of it; she hadn't stolen it.

I'm entitled to a few dreams of my own. Amudha took a deep breath and swallowed her secret, burying it deep inside her.

*

Kannan lay in a stupor in a corner of the one-room tenement, his mind clouded by an alcoholic haze. Waves of the cheap white palm toddy he had drunk rose from him. He stank of stale sweat drying on his unwashed body. Amudha looked at him as she would at a bowl of rice gone sour in the heat of the midday sun. But it would take more than a drunken father to dampen the wellspring of joy inside her. Life to her was like a heavily laden mango tree. You had better reach out and pluck the best moments before they were gone. And so her mind turned to the popular jig she'd watched on a TV show last night. Her feet throbbed. Right and left and right three times, left and right and spin around...

The weight of a heavy blow cracked into her head as she turned.

'Do you know what the time is? Move... Go to work. Stop behaving as if you're the dance director in the movies, okay?' Selvi's face was a mottled red, her rounded eyes hot coals of ire.

She stabbed a finger in Kannan's direction. 'He lies there drunk half the time, and wastes my hard-earned money... never bothers about where the next meal is coming from. And now you stand there swaying your hips. Out, out, off you go. Do you hear me, girl?' Selvi grabbed Amudha's shoulder and shoved her out of the shanty. The girl fled to the safety of Akka's house.

Selvi sighed, wondering when she would see and feel the damp, crushed forty rupees Kannan tucked into his lungi folds at the end of a day at the construction site. It was the corner arrack shop which saw the colour of that money. All Kannan had to show for a day's hard labour was a tipsy gait. Just as soon as his employers caught on to the real reason for his erratic appearances, the job would be gone. If Selvi dared to question him, he cuffed her. When Amudha got in the way, he threw a few punches at her. Artfully Amudha dodged these blows as she did the dark clouds that loomed, dark and threatening, on her horizon. She let her mind roam the realm of pleasant fantasies where the impossible would become possible.

In a family where her father brought home nothing but shame, and mother scraped the bottom to put food on the table, Amudha had acquired a shrewd sense of money management. The Nescafe tin was a secret no one could be trusted with. Hidden away in a rusty trunk under layers of old clothes and scraps of material, it sent out delightful shivers that touched the little girl in unexpected moments. The temptation tugged at her when she was home alone. She would give in to the pull, open the lid gingerly, lift the tin, and jingle its contents close to her ear, a fever of anticipation gripping her. The tin's belly continued to fill up steadily. Every Sunday, Amudha poured the notes and coins into her lap, the silver of the coins' textured surface glinting in the fingers of sunlight that stole into the shanty. Then she started to count slowly, carefully. *Ten rupees. Twelve. Fifteen and fifty paise. Eighteen. Twenty and sixty five.* Her fingertips tingled with desire as they sifted through that money. On her way home from work, she often stopped in front of the glass-fronted displays at the corner store, and ogled the row upon row of lipsticks that sat in their attractive cases. Were there really so many colours? How was it possible to mix so many magical shades? It dazzled her imagination.

In the coming weeks she could think of little else. It was as if a rainbow had crashed into her heart and spilt its colours, colours that swirled inside her head as she swabbed floors and washed sheets.

Two days later Mrs. Ramani set a tall pile of school uniforms, trousers, and starched saris before her and said, 'I'll pay you twenty rupees for this but I want them pressed well.' As the lightweight steam iron wove over the fabric straightening creases, sighing and hissing all the while, an inexplicable joy bubbled inside Amudha. *The twenty rupees would make up the difference.* She was so close to the coveted crimson lipstick. It would be hers tomorrow.

A smile softened her lips as she played out the scenario in her head.

Clutching the treasure tin close, she walks up to the big store that stocks cosmetics. She is standing there, finger on chin, surveying the row of lipsticks just like the well-dressed customers do. Then, in the manner of someone who has considered her choices and finally made up her mind, she strolls over to the sales assistant and points to the lipstick she's craved for the longest weeks of her young life. The sales assistant suppresses a smirk and tries to ignore her. But she soon realises that the girl has no intention of leaving without that lipstick so she tries to embarrass her with: 'You know how much that thing costs?!' And Amudha, with a triumphant flourish, produces the Nescafe tin and tips out its stored secret, the coins chasing each other, winking and twinkling under the spotlights of the store's display counter. Blanching, the assistant hastily gathers it all up and starts to count, her lips moving silently. She picks up the lipstick case and hands it to Amudha.

Sliding her fingers along the sleek, polished surface of the case, Amudha steps out of the store, head held high, a quick smirk at the open-jawed assistant...

*

Stealing into the shanty she crept towards the tin trunk, her body taut, her instincts on high alert. She lifted the lid of the trunk noiselessly, and slid her fingers through the layers of junk until they found the tin and closed around it. She picked it up, and felt its weight with a full heart. Prising its lid off she stared at the mound of coins and the few notes that lay crushed and folded on the side. Heart hammering, she started to tip it into her palm.

That was the moment she felt hot breath on her neck. She spun around and stifled a scream, hand over mouth, her eyes wide with terror.

'Give it to me,' he whispered, baring his stained teeth.

'No!' She moved the hand that held the tin behind her swiftly.

'Give it to me... or you know what I...'

'No, I won't.'

'I'm asking you nicely. Give it to me...' The silken words were threaded with threat.

'No, no, no.' Amudha clung to her dream with her fingertips. At that point his voice cracked.

'I need a drink. Here, look at me.' He held out his shaking hands so his daughter could see the tremors of withdrawal.

Amudha turned her head away.

'I must have a drink… this minute… Just look at me… look… here…' His hands were leaves in a storm.

Amudha clutched the tin.

'No… I won't give this… you can't take it…' Her voice, edged with a touch of hysteria, was beginning to quaver.

'If you don't give me that money right now, you'll be sorry… you'll be sorry all your life. Just look at how I'm shaking. Give it to me… or I'll make your life more miserable than it already is… I'm warning you…'

And he lunged for the tin in a surprise move.

'No… no…' Amudha pivoted away and clung to the tin with every ounce of energy she could muster.

'Give that to me.' He had her in a vice-like grip now and they struggled, swaying from side to side, he desperately trying to loosen her grasp on the tin, she resisting his attempt. Catching him by surprise Amudha used her elbow to deliver a swift kick in his ribs, managed to free herself and flew out of the house as fast as she could.

'You'll regret this… you'll remember this all your life, you witch…' She left the words further and further behind as she ran, the wind in her hair, the Nescafe tin safe in her hands. She didn't stop until she reached the big store.

*

Ten minutes later, tiny bubbles of joy were exploding inside Amudha's heart. She couldn't stop smiling. She twisted the lipstick in and out of its case, marvelled at its creamy texture, held it under her nose and took a deep sniff. Intoxicated by its perfume she skipped homeward, the scene of a moment ago already forgotten. She couldn't wait to slide the lipstick from its case and taste its moist scent on her lips. The tight knot of whispering people hardly pierced her world as she neared home.

She saw it as soon as she stepped into the shanty.

On a long white *dhoti* suspended from the ceiling fan hung Kannan's lifeless form.

The Saint of Lost Things

JOAN PINTO

He was a tiny bald man standing in a five-inch little glass case. That's how we saw him as kids. Grandma's statue of St Anthony was a plaster of Paris figurine, slightly smaller than her palm. He came with a brown robe and staff.

'He's the saint of lost things,' she said as she patted his bald head absent-mindedly, 'when you lose anything, pray to him and you'll find it.'

His head came off at the neck—Grandpapa had accidentally dropped him. Grandma hadn't bothered to stick it back, letting it rest loosely on the torso. When she misplaced something, she would remove the statue from the case, wrap the head in a handkerchief and tell him she wouldn't give it back till she found whatever she had lost.

And she misplaced things as frequently as the crow cawed. Her property papers, recipe book, her rosary, her spectacles that she carried around but didn't really use... But she trusted him like she trusted flour to rise, the sun to come up and Grandpapa to come home drunk. The magic thing was that she always found whatever she lost.

Once when she lost her keys, she prayed to St Anthony, then she wrapped his head in a corner of her *pallo*. He hung there in a bundled knot for two days as she went about her work. It wasn't like she didn't look for the keys. She did. On the second evening after she'd finished making the *chapatis* for dinner, she found them. At the bottom of the *chapati* basket! Maybe she'd put them there amidst distracted chattering to Grandpapa about the new baking oven she'd bought. But it didn't matter how she'd come to lose or find what she did. She praised the bald-headed saint to high heavens, and made sure she bought a garland of lilies on the way home from the market.

I would stand by the Chester drawer and stare at the statue whose face was lit up by the lights of many thin candles. Sometimes I felt he was smiling at me. But *I* never smiled back. I was Grandma's favourite grandchild and it bothered me that she paid so much attention to a statue.

Then one summer day when she was feeding the chickens outside, I hid him, the statue. In the flour tin. Right at the bottom.

She didn't sleep that night. I saw her toss and turn as she lay next to me, sitting up in bed several times to stare at the altar. In the morning she told me she had a dream. She saw St Anthony in a white robe instead of his usual brown one, and he was sneezing. I laughed with her, but felt fear snake up to the back of my neck. I put St Anthony back on the wooden shelf only after I made sure I washed him clean.

Grandma did not bother St Anthony to hunt for every little thing that went missing. But when she couldn't find her gold chain, never mind St Anthony, the entire house was turned upside down. She went hysterical, asking everyone if they'd seen it. Even the milkman; he smoked on the verandah after his rounds and gave her all the news within a one-kilometer radius.

She'd worked hard, tending chickens, selling coconuts and chickoos from the trees she'd planted years ago, to buy that chain. It had taken her six years, and it was all she had to her

name—the most beautiful chain I had seen. It was made up of
bright gold beads and looked like a rosary. She'd worn it just
once. To the Bandra fair and to mass at Mount Mary's Church
afterwards—the big event that happened once a year. After that
she'd put it in the cupboard and locked it away safely to be
pulled out later for a wedding or church feast.

The police were brought in and everyone was questioned.
We knew it could've been one person: my oldest second cousin.
He was twenty-two, twelve years older than me, and sometimes
we called him uncle. He'd almost gone to jail once for belonging
to a gang of petty robbers. But he denied it.

St Anthony's head was wrapped in a handkerchief wet from
tears and slipped under a pillow. Everyday she took him out and
spoke to him like an errant son who wasn't fulfilling his duty to
his parents. A week and a half later, my aunt Greta found the
chain inside an old vase she'd pulled out to clean. No one knew
how it got there, but St Anthony found his place back on the
altar.

Then one day Grandma's youngest son and my uncle,
twenty-nine-year-old Carlton went missing. He was last seen at
the railway station where the Central-line trains began their
journey. She waited a day, two days, but there was no news. She
took St Anthony with her to the police stations, the hospitals,
the railway stations, carrying him along in her threadbare handbag,
refusing to have anyone tagging along. 'I'm not old yet,' she said.
She came home in the evenings a little more defeated than the
day before. But even then, she believed in St Anthony. I saw her
sitting by herself in front of the altar, the flames from the candles
haloing her wrinkled face. She held the statue in soft fleshy
hands, her tears falling on his face, becoming his.

In the days that followed she became quieter than I ever knew her to be. She didn't even yell at me if I walked over the wet floor minutes after she'd swabbed it, or chased her beloved chickens. A month later, in the early hours of a summer morning, before the crows began their cawing, she died. In her sleep. Just like that. Bronchi… something… lung fatigue, the doctors said. I knew it was actually her heart that got tired.

A policeman came home that afternoon. A body had been found, a little outside the city. They thought it could be Carlton. Would someone go identify it?

It *was* Carlton. He had died at about six a.m. the medical reports said. About the same hour Grandma left.

Maybe she did find him after all. In another place. Then again, maybe not. Even so, she was buried within reach of her youngest son. In the very next grave, in the shadow of a neem tree. So that she'd rest, content in the knowledge that she'd been right in her faith. That he had never failed her, that gentle saint who stands on the altar, the wax from many candles making a pool at his feet.

An Offering

TULSI BADRINATH

Laurie Danner had invited Gowri home for Christmas but left Mayberry earlier than planned when her mother fell ill. Gowri had a sense of great escape. Then, at Easter she invited Gowri again and this time, Gowri found an excuse not to go. Over summer she had offered twice to return to the campus, just to pick Gowri up and drive her to Riverside.

Gowri was nonplussed by the invitations Laurie pressed on her. They were friendly with each other in class, but never met downtown in the evenings nor spoke frequently on the phone. Laurie had not invited her even once to the off-campus apartment she shared with her fiancé, yet she was keen on taking Gowri all the way home to Riverside. Gowri did not understand.

When another invitation came her way in September, just before the Fall Quarter began, she did not have the courage to say no. She accepted Laurie's invitation to spend three days with her family. They would return in time for the first day of classes.

Laurie generously offered Gowri the use of her mother's washing machine to do her laundry. It was tempting; Gowri would save at least two dollars if she took her laundry to be washed at the Danners' home. Her bedsheets felt limp, almost oily, but the end of the month, when she usually washed them, was still far away. She could do her windcheater as well. But how would it look, arriving at Laurie's home with loads of dirty clothes, chaddis and all? What would the Danners, especially

Laurie's mother, think of her? Realizing, with rueful pride, that she hadn't adapted entirely to American ways, she left her laundry behind.

The morning was bright and sunny as they set off. After much thought, Gowri wore her best pair of black jeans for the trip. Laurie had a car with some sort of automatic control, so that she drove with her left leg folded on the seat, right foot on the pedal and both thumbs placed casually on the lower part of the steering wheel. Gowri, who knew nothing about driving, and had seen no one else drive in a similar way, was in a state of alarm the entire length of the journey.

Laurie had grown up in the small town of Riverside, gone to school there, and had dated her fiancé Tom since high school. They both attended Mayberry University. Laurie's grandmother, on her father's side, hadn't been told that Laurie and Tom lived together in Mayberry. She would not approve, said Laurie. It had something to do, Gowri gathered, with Laurie's grandmother being Catholic, while the rest of the family was Baptist.

Laurie's father had died some years ago. She had two brothers and a sister, all of whom lived within a little distance of each other and their mother. This ensured that though Mrs Danner lived alone in the family house, her children and grandchildren were near her and visited her almost every day. They were, Gowri understood, a close-knit family.

As Laurie drove through the countryside, her sneakered foot now planted on the seat, bent knee raised window-level, the farms on either side fell away and they climbed a hill. Past a bend, Gowri saw rows of white crosses gleaming austerely in a field of well-tended grass. Here and there, flowers shed colour on stone slabs. It took a while for Gowri to realize they were passing a graveyard, a cemetery. Open to the sun and the breeze, and the ethereal blue above, hanging closer here on the hill, it didn't look scary at all.

'My father's buried here,' said Laurie matter-of-factly as they drove past the cemetery. 'We come and visit him on Memorial Day.'

Gowri craned her neck to look back. What would it feel like to leave one's father here, passing every now and then? Right now, was Laurie remembering him as he had been when alive, only lying beneath the ground, or was she thinking of bones dressed in cherished but disintegrating fabric? She felt for Laurie but did not know what to say. After all, it had been some years since he had died. The trip had much potential for embarassment; what she had been apprehensive of was suddenly upon her. There was a brief silence in the car when her mind seemed to have gone completely blank. She was grateful to Laurie when she began talking about the new café that had opened in Mayberry.

On reaching Riverside, Laurie drove down a road with compact, almost-identical houses on both sides. The houses were unfenced. Turning right, she drove up a grassy bank and parked the car to the side of a small white house. There was no garage, they entered by the front door. Acutely aware of the dark colour of her skin, her wavy hair, Gowri found her hands were ice-cold, and she seemed to have forgotten how to breathe properly.

Mrs Danner was a kindly, plain-featured woman. She did not engage Gowri in much conversation. Instead, she busied herself in the kitchen cooking one delicious meal after another for her guest. Showing Gowri how to make pasta from scratch, she introduced her to decobbed corn in a simple sauce, homemade 'pickles' and cornbread and assured her that making wholesome vegetarian meals was not a problem. Soon, Gowri was at ease.

Until then, Gowri's knowledge of everyday life in America was limited to T-5, the flat she shared with Swati and Ruchi. Furniture borne triumphantly away from the dumpster, a mad assortment of crockery and cutlery left behind by previous residents, mattresses that had passed from student to student, all this combined to give T-5 a makeshift quality. It was home but only in the sense of a place one returned to after venturing out into a strange, sometimes forbidding, world. A place of shelter.

The Danners were unpretentious and their house modest. Gowri yielded gladly to the pleasures of a well-kept, proper home. She helped Laurie hang freshly washed clothes on lines strung under a tree in the garden; the sight of them drying in the breeze gave her an inexplicable thrill. Eating Mrs Danner's home-grown tomatoes made her feel happy. Sleeping in a bedroom that actually had a dresser and mirror, curtains, chairs, carpet, and a solid wooden bed skirted by ruffles—seen only in photographs in American magazines— brought her deep delight.

Laurie had the prettiness of youth. She was slim, but gave the impression of being solid, heavy of bone. She wore jeans and a T-shirt most of the time. Her favourite word was 'humongous'. Gowri watched Laurie do her hair in the morning. She had had no idea how elaborate the American toilette was, it was not just applying shampoo and a thorough drying with a towel after. Laurie shampooed, curled, moussed, crimped, and blew dry her blonde hair until she was satisfied with her reflection in the mirror. At the end of all of that, her hair was caught in a ponytail at the back and rose in a froth of curls over her forehead.

Laurie showed her the wedding dress she had picked out of a catalogue, pictures of the kind of cake her best friend was going to make and discussed the colours she was thinking of for the bridesmaids. 'I'll never be able to please all four of them,' she fretted. 'Dress, colour, shoes, accessories,' she counted them off on her fingers, 'it's a nightmare. They'll hate me forever.' She was waiting to graduate and was planning a summer wedding. Gowri was both taken aback and pleased when Laurie told her she was one of just five classmates to be invited to her wedding.

The third morning, wandering about Laurie's house, Gowri hummed *Gayiye Ganapati* to herself. The song surfaced in her mind suddenly and stayed there, so she hummed it the entire morning. It was the fourth of September.

When she left in the afternoon, Mrs Danner gave her a hamper filled with freshly plucked garden tomatoes, a jar of pickled beetroots and lots of cornbread. Touched by this gesture, Gowri thanked Mrs Danner profusely. The change had done her good. If Laurie invited her back, she would accept readily.

At Laurie's home, during those three days Gowri felt a kind of peace, a tranquillity that was absent in Mayberry. The Danners were simple, uncomplicated people. Their world was restricted and their expectations of it were simple as well. Laurie, the youngest, was the only one of her siblings who had gone on to graduate school. She was of average intelligence and had limited ambitions. She would graduate and get married, her husband and she would hunt for a job in one of the bigger cities of Ohio. She had not travelled outside the state except to the malls in West Virginia.

It had taken the trip to Riverside for Gowri to realize something she should have seen much earlier. All the students at the university, with the exception of the few whose parents lived in Mayberry, were away from home. All of them were leading uprooted lives, it was only a matter of degree and distance.

Riverside was a few hours away by car, her home in Bangalore was long hours and the forbidding cost of a ticket away by plane.

Each one of them drew a connection between Mayberry and the world outside. A picture came to her mind of irregular, tangled rays shooting outwards from a glowing nucleus of students, each ray of light ending at their respective homes in the country or across the world.

When Laurie dropped her back at Maple Street, she thought about the song again, wondering why it had come to mind just then, in such an unexpected place as Laurie's home. She remembered that her father had written to her about Ganesh Chaturthi, it fell sometime in September.

Gowri went up to her room, bare except for two box springs-and-mattress crammed into it, and looked through the latest of her parents' letters. With the feeling that something beautiful and strange had occurred, she read the date of Ganesh Chaturthi that year, September the fourth! She had not missed it.

She had a bath and changed into a cotton nightgown. The cupboards in the kitchen were empty of anything that could be made into a sweet *prasâda* instantly. *Patram pushpam phalam toyam...* She took six of Mrs Danner's reddish-orange tomatoes, placing them on the desk to the side of the puja, in offering.

She went downstairs again and filled the two brass diyas she had with oil, carrying them back up carefully. She borrowed a pale blue cotton-ball from her roommate Ruchi's store in the cupboard on the landing and fashioned two lumpy, uneven wicks. She wedged the sharp ends of three agarbatis in the metal grill of the radiator—she did not have a stand—and switched off the lights. It was night.

The lamps were lit and the tips of the agarbatis were like three tiny burning coals. The air filled with sandalwood incense.

After she finished the puja, a colourless, improper puja, without flowers or even leaves, without kumkum and sandalwood paste, without a sweet *prasâda* for the god who was intensely fond of *modaka*s, Gowri sat on the floor and sang with feeling, *Gâyiye Ganapathy jagavandana, Sankara suvana Bhavâni nandana*... As always, by the time she reached the end, she was moved to tears, *Mângata Tulsidâs kara jodé, basé râmasiya mânasa moré.*

In the darkness, their outlines blurred by the tears welling in her eyes, the gods wore the aureole of light thrown by the oil-lamps. She leaned against the wall and looked at the wavering golden flames and the play of light on the rotund belly and the tapering trunk. This very god had granted success to her, sent her to America, clearing all obstacles from her way. He was here with her even if her family was not. Tears slid down her cheeks, wet, warm.

When the flames faltered, hissed, spluttered and died, and the floor was covered with thin curlicues of ash, the burden of memory seemed too great to bear. Dark mixture of coconut and melting jaggery in a steamed rice-flour wrapping. Her grandmother's deft fingers sealing them with perfection while Gowri's were always too big or too small, and the stuffing burst open the soft white envelope. At that stage in the preparations, it always seemed like they were making too few. Only, once the puja was done and she could finally eat them, greedily, one after another, warm softness sweet in her mouth, she would find herself full very soon. And on the floor of the smoky kitchen, beneath a colourful gilt canopy, sat a benign clay figure immersed deep in petals, equally sated.

The click of the flimsy screen-door opening. A key was turned in the slot and the front-door banged shut. Below, voices echoed loudly, there was much laughter. Ruchi and Swati had told her they were bringing home some of the students newly arrived from India. The mood evaporated, thought was no longer possible.

She switched on the lights in the room and began to make a list of the things she would need for the new academic session. The six tomatoes sat on the desk. She would have to wait till the crowd left before going downstairs to eat one as *prasâda*.

There were whispers in the air that a war had begun in the east and was blowing towards the great lake.

The lake people lived in peace and owed no allegiance to either group.

Look!

But they were afraid that the war that raged in the east would envelope their village. For such were the ways of war.

But the war would not come...

... not until twelve egrets flew across the sky, as the ancient prophecy foretold.

So, the lake people waited.

But when the white birds arrived, it was too late.

Runners brought the news that the two warring groups were inching closer and a decisive battle would be fought around their village.

82

Soon, the first band of soldiers arrived. But they walked into an empty village. There was not a pig in sight.

What could have happened? Where were all the people?

And then they saw them in the distance.

Then the battle for the lake began. It was a long one. Other battles followed. And only one or two lived long enough to tell the tale of what they saw...

83

This is an extract from 'The Floating Island', one of the five stories in Parismita Singh's forthcoming graphic novel *The Hotel at the End of the World*. Narrated by the Blind Prophet, 'The Floating Island' is part of an intricate and grander tale.

The Thief

SHAKTI BHATT

Narayani wore a bright green sari with orange flowers, not unlike the African tulips that bloomed on the tree outside our neighbour's house. She stood on the street—our street, littered with tyre-crushed lilacs—speaking broken Malayalam from the black metal gate leading to our house.

'How much for sweeping and mopping?' Grandmother asked, drying her wet, freshly dyed hair with her fingers. 'Everyone here gives 125 rupees but because we have five bedrooms I'll give you 150.'

Narayani, not made uncomfortable by the mention of money, said, 'I'll cook and wash clothes, but I won't clean.'

Grandmother looked meaningfully at me. I was to her left, in our garden, sitting on one of the marble mushrooms Grandfather had installed under the frangipani. Grandfather said it was difficult to see any possibility of softness or colour—or did he say colour and life?—emerging from the frangipani at this time of year. To me, it seemed as if the tree was upside down, its dry roots spread in the air. I did not know what Grandmother meant by that look of hers so I imitated it in reply: I pursed my lips, widened my eyes, and raised my eyebrows. Grandmother needn't have asked Narayani why she wouldn't clean—everyone knew that some maids would not clean other people's houses, particularly their bathrooms; they even kept lower-caste maids to clean their own—but she did.

'No,' was all Narayani said in reply, shaking her head, smiling, hoping she hadn't embarrassed a potential employer. Grandmother ignored her reply.

'What kind of food do you make?'

'Kerala food, Punjabi food...'

'We don't like Punjabi food.'

'I can make Chinese also. Gobi Manchurian, vegetable spring roll, noodles.'

'Will you wash the dishes at least?'

After an hour of negotiating various chores and their reimbursements, it was arranged, and announced, that Narayani would cook lunch and dinner; buy groceries; wash dishes; attend to the door, the three phones, and to sundry errands for family members. She would also be responsible for making tea (with strictly designated quantities of sugar, water, milk, and spices) for us and for those who visited the house. It is impossible to list all the people who came to our house in a day, but I read in one of Grandfather's articles, 'There is inherent nobility in every descriptive attempt, however inadequate.' (I'd never want Grandfather to know I read, much less remembered, something he'd written.) There were men who came to sell milk, coconuts, vegetables, and fruits; the garbage man; the driver; the gardener; Grandfather's peon; at least a couple of relatives and friends, or a reader of Grandfather's columns who was 'just passing by and thought I'd drop in'. Then there were the people who came on a weekly basis: Grandmother's broker and her real estate agent; and on a monthly one: the broad-shouldered Kashmiri carpet and cloth sellers with fair faces and red lips; the cableman and the manager of the trash-collecting service. I am sure I've missed some, like the people who came to collect funds for the parks, the tennis court, the street signs and the like; the odd-job men; relatives and friends of the maids; and the saleswomen in rubber slippers and long-sleeved blouses who sold washing powder and cook books.

Narayani lived twenty miles from the city in a one-room shack, which she cleaned, broomed, and wet-mopped first thing in the morning. Then she made lunch for her family; it was always sambar and rice, and, on a special day, an added spicy vegetable, all of which she mixed and packed in light steel boxes with rubber-coated hooks for her daughters to take to their English-medium school. 'Don't talk in class, and listen to madam,' she said to them when they left the house, their hair tightly plaited with red nylon ribbons. Their father did not get up, if he was home, before one or two in the afternoon. Narayani took the 7.25 bus, which took about an hour to get to our part of town. From the bus stop, she went straight to the Old Lady from the North that lived across the street from us—it was she who sent Narayani to Grandmother when Terrible Birama left.

The Old Lady lived in a two-storeyed box-like house by herself. The building had been painted yellow once. She had sons and daughters who lived abroad and visited her when they were getting married or to show her their children. Three maids other than Narayani came to the Old Lady at different times of day. She told my Grandmother this was a wise thing to do: 'It keeps them reasonable; they don't think your world will collapse without them.'

The first thing Narayani did at the Old Lady's was make tea. She heated a cup of milk with a few spoons of sugar and poured it into a small china cup, whose edges had gathered unwashable lines of dirt. Then she put a Taj Mahal tea bag in the cup, and gave it to the Old Lady in a saucer on a large tray edged with cane. Narayani had her tea at our house; 'taste is not same,' she said, if tea was not boiled. While the Old Lady drank her tea, Narayani gathered the white saris that had been hung to dry on the first-floor balcony, and ironed them. The Old Lady insisted her underwear—also white (she was a widow)—was ironed as well. After the ironing, Narayani gave the woman a massage in a room that I imagined to be very dark because I never saw any electric lights in the house, not even at night.

Narayani often spoke of the massage, and each time she did I tried to imagine the Old Lady naked. She had a strange body. Its shape was like an almond, tapering toward the ends and wide in the middle. Her face and neck had so many layers it reminded me of Sultan, our neighbour's boxer. Once, in the early evening, when Grandmother and I were playing badminton, she stepped outside her house to buy coconut water and I saw her in something other than a sari—a short-sleeved nightgown that reached just below her knees. Her ankles and wrists were small, and though there was hair visible everywhere, fair soft skin lay below it. When she turned, I caught a glimpse of her back. She did not seem to be wearing underwear: two masses of flesh hung some distance below her waist, not far above the back of her knees, and the dress stuck to her as if it was wet. Narayani did not like to massage her because the Old Lady wanted her to go on and on. Sometimes the massage would take a couple of hours. By then, Narayani's hands would become erratic, lose all sense of rhythm and touch. The Old Lady would let another few minutes pass, after which she would say, 'Bas.'

The slam of the kitchen door—enough to scare the koels off the avocado tree—at 10.30 meant Narayani had come. She entered by the back door because Grandmother had asked her not to ring the bell. Grandfather's study was near the front door, adjoining the garden, and he did not like 'frivolous diversions' and 'unnecessary distractions.' He had spent more than forty years of his life working for the government, in the Research and Analysis Wing. It had been a few years since he retired; now he wrote articles on India's intelligence failures for national newspapers. From the kitchen, Narayani walked into the hallway and called to each of us in turn, declaring her presence with customized greetings.

'Amma, what we making today?'

'Baby, you want noodles?'

'Akka, tea for you?'

She knew the answers to all these questions, but she never stopped asking them. The vegetables were rotated weekly between beans, cabbage, lady's finger, long gourd, and green brinjal. We made only three or four types of curries: coconut curry with shrimp and the puli Grandmother grew in the garden; sambar with carrots and drumsticks; curd curry; rasam with as much garlic as tomatoes. There were two kinds of breads: chapatis without ghee, and oily parathas; and two kinds of rice: white and brown Kerala rice, which I did not eat because Grandmother, at every meal, said, 'It is *very* good for you, *full* of vitamin B and potassium.' Narayani also knew I liked Superhit Kishen noodles, which Grandfather called 'poison food', for breakfast during the holidays; I was promised this daily treat by Father if I passed Maths. If I didn't, I would have to resume the three-hour daily tutorials with the teacher who called me by no other word but 'idiot'. Mother, whom Narayani called her elder sister, liked her tea black, without sugar, boiled with a few seeds of cardamom and a thumb-long piece of ginger. Narayani poured three cups into a flask that Mother took to work. Father left home before Narayani arrived.

Because of Grandfather's cholesterol levels Grandmother put almost no oil and salt in the food. Often, I made myself a mayonnaise sandwich with white bread, not Grandfather's organic whole grain that was also '*very* good for you'. Narayani didn't like it when I didn't eat her food. She would wait for Grandmother to step out of the kitchen, which didn't happen very often, then add the forbidden condiments to the food. Grandmother would tell us, and our guests, 'We put no oil or salt in our food and it is still *so* tasty!'

In the kitchen, I liked to stir the vegetables, and fry fish and potato chips. Narayani would grate coconut halves over a serrated steel knife attached to a wooden stand, sitting with her knees raised on either side, or she would cut onions, her eyes pouring forth. At first, she spoke to me in Malayalam and Tamil, and I mixed some of that into my English. Then I started to speak only in English because she was good at getting the gist of what I said. In months, she learnt to understand and speak comprehensible, even if erratic, English. It was inevitable: all of us spoke the language except Grandmother who insisted on talking in Malayalam, even to those who did not understand it, like our poor Kannadiga gardener. Grandfather said how shameful it was that a great language was dying and though he said it to no one in particular, or everyone at once, say in the car on our way back from a dinner, after he had had his customary two rums, I knew his accusation was pointed at me. I was sure Narayani was the only maid in our neighbourhood who said 'You're wellcome,' when you said thanks, and who said 'Esscuse me', when she sneezed, even if there was no one around.

It was spring, almost six months after Narayani came to work for us. That season, each day, Grandfather took me for a drive to look at the laburnums. They bore flowers for only two weeks of the year, he told me. I liked the yellow, bell-like flowers that looked as if they might all fall at once if one were to shake the tree ever so lightly. This was the time of year that Grandmother vacuumed the house. Once a year, she liked to clean the carpets, which were broomed daily by the cleaning maid, a thin, fair woman with dreamy eyes and clean skin, who, unlike her colleague, was reserved in her speech: she replied to everything with a nod or by shaking her head. On a Sunday afternoon, when the rest of us were taking a nap, Grandmother walked into the garage. The vacuum cleaner wasn't there.

It had to be Narayani, Grandmother told me. She was the only one who went into the garage to use the tandoor when we had guests for dinner (every weekend). By this time, Grandmother had become quite used to Narayani, a situation that was not at odds with her constant complaining about her if something was wrong with the cooking: 'This Narayani has not learnt *anything*', and if someone praised it: '*I* put the masala'. Having Narayani around meant Grandmother could go to the weekly meetings and activities of the Ladies' Club of Bangalore; she could watch her favourite show in the morning, even if she watched it with an overpowering restlessness, going into the kitchen during commercials, answering doorbells and phone calls. For some reason, when she watched TV, she was more attentive than ever to what was going on in the house.

'Narayani, I can't find the vacuum cleaner.' They were in the kitchen making lemon-rice and fish curry. Narayani was not unfamiliar with Grandmother's effortful, innocent turn of tone.

'Where did you keep it, Amma?'

'In the garage.'

'It's not there?'

'No. I want to clean the carpets. It's always been right there next to the Maruti.'

'Did you look properly?'

'Yes, Narayani.'

'I'll go look for it.'

'Not now, first finish cooking.'

Grandmother did not think Narayani was lying, though who else could have done it? The other maid never went into the garage. She entered and left by the main door, and she had often returned the limp rupee-notes she found in our clothes. The peon that came to help Grandfather was like family. He ate lunch with us and helped Grandmother in her garden: feeding the ever hungry fish in the lotus tank, turning the soil, picking the papayas and coconuts, watering the lawn, fixing the solar lamps. Even if he had gone up to her and confessed to the crime, say, she would have laughed, slapped him on the back, and said, 'Poda!'

Grandmother wondered whether she should fire Narayani over a superfluous vacuum cleaner. Unlike other big cities, Bangalore—I heard her telling Mother who was about to fire her driver once—did not have a ready supply of unskilled labour: 'Maids, drivers, gardeners, watchmen are not easy to find.' That must have been why we kept that driver who showed up bloody-eyed, unshaved, unwashed, wearing the same brown pants and dirty white T-shirt for three or four days in a row. He insisted on being paid by the day, and his grandmother in a distant village was sick at least every other week. Once found, the workers were hard to keep; they demanded many things other than their salaries. Take the Terrible Birama whom we had to sack. She had demanded a steady supply of brightly coloured gel toothpaste, Parachute coconut hair oil, medium-strength Colgate toothbrushes, and Lux beauty soap. Grandmother drew the line at Fair & Lovely. Birama liked to sleep till seven, which was the time Grandfather liked his breakfast of idli, upma, or puttu, and she watched TV in the dining room, with the volume turned up loud, compounded by her laughing and talking back to the characters on the screen. On a day when Grandmother was out and Birama was watching a movie, we had asked her to make a prawn curry. She nodded her coconut-oiled head and when we came down two hours later, she was still watching the movie. On her return, after being briefed by us on this outrageous behaviour, Grandmother said, 'This will not do, Birama, you find another place.' 'I was going to leave anyway,' Birama said. 'You people shout too much.'

Grandmother looked intently at the frying pan. She asked Narayani to put more turmeric in the rice and, next time, to not use so much oil for the fish. Before leaving the kitchen, she told Narayani that no one liked the biryani she had made the day before because there were far too many chillies in it. That evening Grandmother asked all of us to lock our valuables and not leave money lying around. No one except she and I knew about the stolen vacuum cleaner. (Later, when I told my parents about it, they did not seem to care.) No point telling Grandfather; he would say, 'Why do you always talk of trivial things? When I was your age, I was reading James and discussing Spinoza.' I didn't make the mistake of asking him who these people were.

The month after the vacuum cleaner incident, the cleaning

maid quit. Two of my shirts were found missing. Naturally, we, that is, Grandmother, questioned the maid since she was in charge of washing, drying, folding, and delivering the clothes to our rooms. She didn't say a word, just shook her head. The next day she arrived with a large white plastic bag, so stuffed one couldn't hold its ends together. It contained everything we had given her as gifts for Diwali and Christmas over the years. She left in a week, insisting on working the full month even after Grandmother, feeling betrayed, angry and guilty, had agreed to pay her anyway.

None of us suspected Narayani of taking the shirts. We were too used to her to imagine not having her around. I liked the hour or so that I spent talking to her in the kitchen. Grandmother did not like it because Narayani worked slower when she talked. If she got excited about something, she would drop what she was doing altogether and speak in an English that was as wild as her gesticulations: 'Tell me, baby, what I do with him? I tell him to get out my house but he is not go.'

Soon after the other maid quit, Narayani lost her job at the Old Lady's. One of her younger, unmarried sons had returned from the US to find a wife. One day, he saw Narayani massaging his mother and asked her to do the same for him. She was massaging his legs and arms when he took her hand and put it into his shorts, smiling kindly at her. Narayani went straight to the Old Lady and said, 'Give me money for this month. I don't want to work here.' The Old Lady asked her why and Narayani said, 'Your son behave badly with me.' The Old Lady from the North became very angry, more so because Narayani was speaking in English. She told her never to show her 'dirty black face in this house again'. Narayani lost a monthly income of 300 rupees.

Grandmother told her she would add the amount to her salary if she cleaned our house. Narayani agreed, saying, 'You are like my family. Is okay to clean your house.'

It was summer, but this time I wasn't allowed to eat noodles—I had done badly in the exams. I was reading *The Princess Diaries* when Grandmother came in, as always without knocking. She asked if I had given Narayani a key chain Father got me for my birthday.

'Why?'

'Did you give it to her or not?'

The key chain was attached to a smooth, red, glass heart with watery yellow and blue ribbons inside it. I saw it in a store where Father was buying the weekly race guide and I said I wanted it. He gave it to me as a surprise for my birthday. After using it for a couple of months I put it away. Surprised at my quick understanding, I realized Narayani must have picked it up from one of the dumps in my room, the TV room, or my parents' room.

'I don't remember, why?'

'What do you mean you don't remember? How can you forget such a thing? You people.'

'I gave it to her. Now can you leave me alone?'

'If you gave it to her, how can you forget and then *suddenly* remember? And this is no way to speak to your grandmother.'

It was easy to lie to Grandmother. If she considered most people untrustworthy, she thought her own family incapable of hiding the truth from her. She told me not to give anything to Narayani without asking her, and left the room. Mother told me later that Grandmother had seen a bunch of keys hanging from Narayani's waist. The keychain was tucked inside the skirt of her sari and attached to a hook with steel hearts painted gold. Grandmother's eagle eyes noticed the polished hearts gleaming in the late morning light in the kitchen.

'Narayani, where did you get that keychain?' Grandmother said.

'Baby gave it to me,' Narayani said without blinking.

I started going to school again and I didn't see much of Narayani until the Diwali holidays, when she wore new saris every day. On Bhaiduj, she invited her brother home for lunch and served him three vegetables, two curries, rice and papad, and rice pudding; at the end of the meal she touched his feet and he gave her fifty-one rupees. On Laxmi Puja, Narayani wore a red sari printed with flowers of a darker red; she pinned a few strings of jasmine in her hair. Narayani had dark, unblemished skin that glowed after she washed it with a thick paste of gram flour and milk cream. Her forehead was small, and if you saw her from a distance it looked as if her eyebrows were unseparated. Her eyes were as dark as her hair, and her unusually long lashes made her look much younger than her twenty-eight years. The pink of her lips had faded around the edges. With her high cheekbones, small breasts, slim waist, and strong, lean hands, Narayani looked like a new college student aiming for a degree in Zoology. She wore enough gold to show off her caste: dangling earrings, a mangalsutra—paid for by her, not her husband, a daily reminder of the financial indignity of her marriage—that hung loosely around her neck, another necklace, thicker and tighter, with small red and green stones, studs in her upper ears, glass bangles that matched her sari, two anklets, which composed different melodies depending on the work she performed, and two or three toe rings. For all four days of Diwali, she wore on her forehead an uneven blot of red powder mixed with a few grains of rice. One day she arrived long after noon. She had given lunch to the girls in her neighbourhood, she said.

'Five girls who are not married, I give them lunch. Before they leave I give one steel bowl, one jasmine gajra, one blouse piece.'

'Did you do that also for your husband?'

Narayani missed lunch on Tuesday for her husband's health and avoided meat on Friday so god would find her husband a job.

'No, this is for my daughters so they get a good husband.'

'Like yours,' I teased her.

'No, not like my husband, baby, why you say like that?'

There was only a month to Christmas. Grandmother had begun preparations: shopping for the ingredients that went into her famous plum cake; assembling the tree and its decorations; buying gifts for those who would attend our annual party and cards for relatives who lived abroad. At this time of year, Grandfather's work seemed to increase, and at night he listened with practised disinterest to Grandmother's updates. He would be in charge of the bar at the Christmas party. He always took great care to mix the exact proportions of water, tonic, soda or fruit juice to the various liquors. He never used lemons: 'Only people who don't know anything about drinking use lemons.' He stocked imported stuffed olives and cocktail mixes; three cabinets in the living room stood ready with glassware that he used only for the Christmas dinner.

It was a week before the party when Grandmother walked into the kitchen and asked Narayani to come to her bedroom. I was helping her stir-fry vegetables and she was telling me about the TV her mother's employer had given the family. It had been lying unused for months, Narayani said, because her mother could not afford the monthly cable fee of 250 rupees. Her neighbours were planning to chip in so the women could watch their favourite soaps, and the men, cricket. When she reappeared from the bedroom a few minutes later, it was with a preoccupied expression on her face. But she continued to work, her eyes giving nothing away.

'So are you going to pay too?'

'Ya.'

'How much?'

'Ten rupees.'

After that she didn't say a word; I ran to Grandmother. Grandfather's pink diamond ring was missing. Great Grandmother had given the ring to him on his twenty-fifth wedding anniversary. She had taken the ring to the church at Velankanni where it was 'blessed by Mother Mary for peace and prosperity in marriage'. Grandmother told this story to whoever praised the ring. It was a rectangular diamond held by four thin gold claws. Around it on a circular frame, also gold, were twenty-one minute white diamonds (I counted them). Grandfather's mother had died a few months after their anniversary, so the ring bore added value. Grandfather wore it along with his engagement and wedding rings, and another white stone ring that was given to him when he was very young to shape his temper.

Grandfather was in the habit of placing the ring on the counter of the washbasin each time he used it. The day before Grandmother found it missing, he had forgotten to put the ring back on. He remembered it only that night. Grandmother was in the kitchen, rinsing and stacking the dinner dishes. When she came into the bedroom she noticed he was more talkative than usual. For the first time in many months, he asked if she was tired.

'Oh, of course not. It's *nothing*. How was your work today?'

'It was OK. I wanted to finish something I'm working on but I wasn't able to.'

She took a sleeping pill—she had been taking one for as long as I could remember—and they went to bed. He waited for her to fall asleep. This took a long time: she didn't hear him snore so she wondered what was bothering him. Hours after they had occupied their ends of the bed, Grandfather called out Grandmother's name, first softly, then boldly. He got up and looked for the ring in the bathroom, in the closet, in the kitchen—where he had gone to get custard apple ice cream, which he didn't eat for dinner because he was scolding me for having only chocolate ice cream for my meal—in his car, and even in the garage, where he never went. He wondered how to break the news to his wife. He knew, like the rest of us, that a lost item became for Grandmother a call for an entrenched battle with the perceived perpetrator of the crime. The announcement of the loss was followed by hours, sometimes days, of recrimination at the carelessness of the loser. The whole house was put on alert, the servants ruthlessly questioned; and threats of contacting the police were made.

This time the maid under investigation was Narayani. By now the areas of comfort that she provided Grandmother had increased considerably. She gave her the massage that Grandmother had always envied the Old Lady from the North, as well as a head rub and hot towel treatment three times a week. Still, Grandmother was quite upset about the ring, and it was out of the question to overlook it like she had the vacuum cleaner, the shirts, or the keychain, which by now she was convinced had also been stolen. She considered going to the police but could not bear the thought of them entering Narayani's house while her daughters were present. Once, when I was away, Narayani had brought her younger daughter to meet Grandmother. She took a liking to the girl who 'had beautiful eyes. Must have got them from her *father*.' Grandmother also liked the fact that the girl refused everything she was offered: chocolates, biscuits, chips, my ragged Barbie dolls, even the chance to watch TV in my room. '*Such* a nice girl!'

For the next few days Grandmother was unusually quiet, though she continued to supervise arrangements for the party. We had been anticipating a hullabaloo of the most unpleasant kind but it had been a few days and she had said nothing. She told me not to spend time in the kitchen anymore. On one of those days, Narayani came in to clean my room. I was studying for a moral science exam. The frangipanis were finally in bloom and through my windows I could see several clusters of bright flowers, diffused yellow and pink, hanging at the very end of a branch. Grandfather always asked me to wash my hands after I plucked a frangipani flower: the thin white fluid was poisonous; 'That is why no birds come to this tree.' I couldn't help asking Narayani how she was doing. She said her husband told her he was leaving her. 'He go to another woman. She give him more money. I give him hundred every week. She will give him one-fifty rupees.' I asked her why she was unhappy at losing a husband who beat her and her daughters. 'You not understand, baby,' she said, and left the room.

Later that day, over lunch, I heard Grandmother talking to

Narayani in the kitchen—their first conversation in many days. 'You know, Narayani, that ring we lost some days ago? It brings good luck *only* to the person it is given to. If someone else wears it, that person's marriage is destroyed. I pray to god that *nothing* bad happens to whoever has the ring.' I couldn't hear Narayani's reply. Maybe she said nothing. She had begun to look different. Her eyes were dull. She tied her hair in a way that made her look much older. Many times her blouse or bangles didn't match her sari. She had also put on weight around her stomach. The day after Grandmother's talk, Narayani looked as if she had been crying. Her eyes were an ill mix of red and yellow. She said her husband had left her and taken their older daughter with him. When I went into the kitchen, I saw Grandmother rubbing Narayani's back as she wept. Later, Narayani made tea for everyone, then lunch—okra curry, dry spinach with cumin and garlic, and fried mackerel.

The next morning, when Grandmother was teaching me subsets, we heard a shout: 'Amma, look what I found!' Grandmother calmly put her pen down and left the room. In her bedroom, a shiny piece of metal lay on the lower mattress of the bed, near the wooden footboard. Narayani was holding up the mattress with both her hands, her face engaged in an effort to show extreme surprise and elation. The afternoon sunlight that filtered through the cotton curtains split the pink diamond into several hundred pieces, and in it I could see traces of striking blue and purple.

POETRY

TEMSULA AO

Nowhere Boatman

The riders on my boat often ask me
how long I have plied this trade
on the river between
the land of the living
and the land of the dead.

They even ask me
how old I am,
as if knowing my age
has anything to do with their being
on my boat for their last ride
from the land of the living.

But on some slack days I feel like
telling them to go ask
the sky who sees it all
or the wind who hears it all
and even the river itself
who has borne countless others
like them across.

If some persist on prying
I shall send the pesky souls
to the tree-stump whose belly
is now my boat, to tell them
how old is old?

Anyway, what has age to do with dying
and of what use this irrelevant knowledge
when they are already pledged
on a one-way journey
to their destiny?

But at times it worries me;
no one has enquired
who I am and of which clan
and most important of all
where I belong:
the land they have left
or the one they are going to?

A soul without a status,
is how I see myself
fated to ply my trade
on this designated route.

On such depressing days I jingle
the miserable pile of small coins*
that litters the pit of my boat
and ask myself

---

*According to traditional Ao-Naga belief, the souls of dead people have
to pay some coins to the boatman on the river between the Land of the
Living and the Land of the Dead to ferry them across to the other side,
where, it is believed, they begin another existence.

what advantage
this petty exchange
for the un-remitting service
of re-locating well-defined souls
in pre-ordained spaces?

when my own immaterial
existence knows not
whether it can claim
any kinship with the living
or one day join the dead
on a final crossing.

Yet I continue to exist,
an ageless, nameless
indispensable anomaly,
the nowhere boatman
on the river between
two irreconcilable worlds.

The Spear

It was the spear that started it all.

I had to go back for it
To the shed in the jhum
And when I regained the main path
The others were long gone.

At the stream I stood hesitant
On the tree-trunk lying across,
But its cool waters inviting, I waded in
For a quick soak in its wet fold
Before the long trek home.

In the embrace of the soothing fluid
Weariness left my tired limbs
And I came out a new man
My mind bent on home and
The one waiting there.

The shadows were lengthening
As the rays of the fading sun
Sped through bushes and shrubs
Along the rough-hewn jungle path.

With the spear as my only companion
I hurried my pace
When suddenly a low bark
Stopped me in my track.

Another low moan and a blurry flight
Across the path and my spear fled
With lightning speed.
No volition, only instinct accelerating
Deadly aim towards the shapely silhouette

A thud and a crash in the shrubs
And afterwards, a great stillness.

I crept forward and gasped at the sight
Of a writhing doe, my spear firmly
Impaled in her wounded bigness.
Her life ebbing away

She exhaled with a last moaning heave
Expelling new life from her dying frame
Wrapped in her guts and the birthing blood.
She tried to free her new-born
From its watery fold
But my spear stood unyielding in its hold

Grief engulfing my suddenly
Tired body, I stood there numb
A mute witness to my own crime
Until, the evening shadows urged for safety.

Hurriedly gathering some wild grass
I covered her unseeing teary eyes
To mark my shame and invoke
Nature's forgiveness.

Next I erected the circle of 'genna'*
Around the still and bloody duo
Praying fervently that other predators
Would know the sign and steer
Clear of the spear-blighted spot.

Leaving my accursed weapon where it stood,
I ran and stumbled.
Fearful of other demons stalking me
I ran faster, bleeding and weeping
Until I stumbled into the waiting arms
Sitting by the roaring hearth.

As she cradled my tortured self
In the stillness of the night,
I caressed her rounded fullness
Praying to the gods

To protect my seed
From mindless stalkers
Such as me

For now I knew
It was not the spear alone
That caused it all.

---

*It is a word which may mean several things: unclean, sacred, as well as taboo, all meanings indicating prohibition of some sort. The practice of 'genna' has been a part of Naga rituals observed on many different occasions.

NOOREEN SARNA

Bouquets

And because my bouquets are withered
They are not kept on your table,
You do not keep the winter evening on your table.

And because you shield yourself with beauty,
We are kept at a distance even here;
Not even thoughts can linger here.

And because no one has marked your wall,
There are miles of exquisiteness,
But no art in your beauty.

And your miles are not dusty—like mine.

Mediterranean Siesta

Your pickled lemons are now deliciously tangy,
Not heartstopping sour like before,
And so are my regrets.

And the lapping sea brings salt
And takes it away,
Slowly and deliberately,
Continuous like you.

But I have faith in my Mediterranean siesta,
As much as you have in my folded pain,

And before your anxious night,
And after your poisonous day,
I will seal another bottle with oil
And floating scorpion stings.

Refuge

You frequent oriental haunts of strange design,
Twisted rooms furnished with broken brides,
When I poach your wilted mind.

This morning is crippled in your dreams,
The stifling heat of stagnation leaves
The paint on her face, smudged.

Today I will meet you,
And in a trench coat full of keys, coins and cards
I will be stared at,
As if it is *I* who disgraces the morning.

I will risk it to see your crumpled face
And the decadent squalor,
And to justify how rigid I've become.

Notes on Contributors

Temsula Ao has contributed a number of articles on oral tradition, folk songs, myths and cultural traditions of the Ao Nagas and linguistic diversities of the Naga tribes for journals like *Indian Literature* published by the Sahitya Akademi, *Indian Horizons: Journal of the Indian Council for Cultural Relations* etc. She is Professor in the department of English, North Eastern Hill University, Shillong and also Dean, School of Humanities and Education at NEHU. She was awarded the Padma Shri in 2007.

Tulsi Badrinath, born in 1967, lives in Chennai. She has a Bachelor's degree in English Literature and an MBA. Her poems and articles have appeared in various newspapers and journals. Her unpublished novel 'The Living God' has been longlisted for the Man Asian Literary Prize 2007. Tulsi learnt Bharatanatyam from a very young age and has performed widely in India and abroad. She quit her job as a manager in a bank to devote herself to dance and writing. Currently, she is working on a novel and a collection of short stories.

Jahnavi Barua trained as a doctor but is now a writer, a reader, a mother of a six-year-old and a wife, not necessarily in that order. She writes mainly short fiction. She writes because she cannot help it; she writes because she reads; she writes because she is otherwise largely speechless.

Jahnavi is from Assam in the North-East of India and is

passionate about the land she comes from; it has a way of creeping into almost all her works.

In 2005 she had won the Short Fiction contest hosted by Unisun Publishers and the British Council. The following year she won second prize in the Children's Fiction category of the same prize. In 2006, Jahnavi was also awarded a Charles Wallace Trust Fellowship to study Creative Writing in the UK. She lives in Bangalore.

Shakti Bhatt's award-winning short stories have appeared in journals and anthologies in India and the U.K. 'The Thief' won the 2005 Toto Funds the Arts Award for short fiction. Shakti was working on three novels when she died in early 2007. She was 26.

Uma Girish is an internationally published writer whose articles and features have been published in 7 countries. Uma's short fiction has won her several awards, the most recent being e-Author 7.0, India's Largest Online Talent Search. 'Voices Across Boundaries', 'Lunch Hour Stories', 'India Currents' and 'Espresso Fiction' are some of her fiction credits. She is also a Business English trainer and lives in Chennai with her husband and 14-year-old daughter.

Mridula Koshy makes her home in New Delhi. In the past she was a Union and Community Organizer in the United States but threw this over for the lucre and glamour of a career mothering her three. She has been published in the Canadian journal *Existere* and in the Zubaan Books anthology of new writing, titled *21 under 40*. Her work is also forthcoming in the English literary journal, *Wasafiri*, in an anthology of Indian stories published by Saqi press in London and in an anthology of urban Indian writing to be published by the Italian imprint, *ISBN*.

Vijay Parthasarathy, 27, grew up in Bombay. Currently based in Madras, he writes for *The Hindu*.

Joan Pinto grew up in Bombay. She's been an engineer, copywriter and interior designer. Joan has written for a host of publications including *The Times of India, Femina, Design Today, India Today Travel, The CS Monitor*, Boston, and *Gulf News*. Her short fiction 'The Wretched and the Loved' appeared on *Long Story Short*, the e-zine, and a flash memoir 'The Scent of Sawdust' on *flashquake*. Her short story 'How Rifka Made Things Right' was published in *Favourite Stories for Girls* (Puffin).

When Joan is not writing she blows bubbles with her niece, studies the colours in people, runs an NGO, sips chai, hums off-key, wanders through graveyards, and travels. She can be contacted at huanita@yahoo.com or on www.joanpinto.wordpress.com.

Neel Kamal Puri was born in Ludhiana, Punjab, in 1956. She grew up in the erstwhile princely state of Patiala. Since 1979, she has worked as a lecturer in English Literature at different colleges in Patiala and Chandigarh. She is currently teaching Literature and Media Studies at the Government College for Girls, Chandigarh.

Nooreen Sarna is a sixteen-year-old student, a keen environmentalist and the winner of the Asian Age Poetry competition (August 2006).

Parismita Singh is currently working on a graphic novel.

Kishore Valicha has written poetry and short stories that have been published in *New Quest* and earlier in the *Writers' Workshop Miscellany*. His doctoral dissertation on Indian cinema, which later was published in book form, received a National Award from the Government of India. He has written two biographies for Penguin India on Ashok Kumar and Kishore Kumar.